# MEN of COAL

*Edmund Birchall*

## Edmund Birchall

First published in the United Kingdom in 2016 by
Mosaic (Teesdale) Ltd, Snaisgill, Middleton-in-Teesdale,
County Durham DL12 0RP

ISBN 9780993597015

Design, layout and typesetting by
Mosaic Design and Print, Middleton-in-Teesdale.

**From the author**

**Legal Disclaimer**

In writing this novel my goal was to give a realistic impression of the life in coal
mines, in the course of which I make reference to various bodies such as the
National Coal Board, National Union of Mineworkers, the Conservative and Labour
Parties and the Government, and events surrounding those organisations.

The book is based upon my personal experiences, incidents and memories of my
years as a working miner, however, as will be readily understood by the reader, the
novel from start to finish is entirely a work of my imagination, and the characters,
organisations and their actions in the story entirely fictional.

Any other resemblance to actual persons, living or dead, is entirely coincidental.

**Note**

As stated above, all the names and characters are fictional except that of
Bickershaw Colliery, which was a large mine in the Leigh area.

I use the real name because of the tale of the 'Apprentice pulling a cat across the
canal." This story has been told many times in the Leigh area, and I do not attempt
to claim any ownership of it. It has been passed on from generation to generation
and has now become folk legend in the Leigh and Wigan area. I myself was told
this story by a blacksmith from Bickershaw Colliery.

# DEDICATION

The idea of the character of Dan,
although fictional, was influenced by my late
father-in-law – a hard-working foreman
blacksmith – who was a quiet, honest man with
a sharp brain and a unique inventive skill to
develop large-scale working devices with ease.

He also smoked full-strength cigarettes.

I dedicate this book to him.

# One

Roundall was a huge man; he had strong, muscular arms and a rugged face, which often smiled, revealing a perfect set of white teeth.

He sat on his haunches on the coalface in complete darkness.

The only light came from his cap-lamp, which he had switched to the small bulb to save the battery's energy. He could smell the familiar musty smell of the mine air. The silence was occasionally interrupted by the creeking and groaning of the strata and pit props.

He was dressed in just his shorts, socks and clogs, as Redman's mine was deep and hot. His body was shiny black due to the coal dust in the air sticking to the sweat on his body.

A pearl of sweat ran down from his forehead, trickling down his nose to drop on his muscular thigh, and produce a snowflake effect in the matt black coal dust-covered skin.

The collier smiled at the beauty and fascination of the pattern, made as a direct result, of his physical efforts.

Roundall was having a minute.

He was a collier working on No.5 Trencherbone, a four-foot seam at Redman's colliery.

Funny name for a pit, he thought. He reflected about the time when he had once told a young lass he fancied that he worked at Redman's, and she had thought he worked as a shop assistant, selling sliced bacon at one of Redmond's chain of grocery shops in Wigan.

No, his pit was a proper pit, not one of those poncy, shallow, drift mines. It was said that Redman's had the deepest shaft in the country, although, there was some debate as to which pit was the deepest – Redman's, or a nearby colliery in Leigh – but his was a full mile underground, with at least an hour's walk from pit bottom to the coal face.

The pit was located between the towns of Wigan and Leigh, in the Lancashire coalfield.

Roundall was one of the Manager's best, and unbeknown to Roundall, one of his favourite face workers.

It was the 1950s, and coal was still being handfilled, however face mechanisation was slowly creeping in.

It was Monday morning, and Roundall had just shifted five of his allocated ten tons of coal, or 'breyd', as it was called down there.

He pulled the top off his tin drinking can and took a long drink of the cool, clear water, feeling it gush down the inside of his throat. He then carefully replaced the lid and tied it on a support bar with an old piece of shot-wire, because drinking-water down a mine is precious.

Roundall picked up his large pear-shaped shovel, adjusted his knee-pads and scrambled on his knees back to his breyd.

The four foot thick coal in the Trencherbone seam was good quality household coal. It had been undercut by a Samson coal cutter during the previous nightshift.

At the start of his shift Roundall had passed the nightshift machine men. On his way to the coalface he'd seen big Andy from Leigh and little Dave from Ince. Dave had the reputation of being able to drink a crate of Guinness in one night.

Following the undercutting, and just before the dayshift started, the shot-firer had stemmed the pre-drilled holes with cartridges of Nobel explosives. From a safe distance he then exploded the charges to bring the coal crashing down, to await the following dayshift arrival of Roundall and his team of twenty colliers.

The coalface was about two hundred yards, with ten yards to a man. That's about ten tons each in seven hours. Hard physical and dirty work.

The shaker pans suddenly started up. These were like long metal troughs and looked like a long children's slide. They moved in a jerky motion, backwards and forwards about a foot each way, and produced a loud shrieking noise. The movement caused the coal, which had been shovelled onto them by the colliers, to slide down towards the main gate roadway. From there it went out on towards the pit bottom by conveyor belts and was eventually deposited into tubs, which were sent by rope haulage to the pit bottom.

Roundall positioned himself comfortably on his knees, and started to shovel the large lumps of coal onto the shaker pans, gradually building up a steady rhythm.

After two hours of solid effort, and with his body shiny black with sweat, Roundall saw in the distance a light from a cap-lamp and a safety lamp dragging towards him. He knew this would be Tommy Green, the mine undermanager.

Tommy, because of his eccentric nature, and his undermanager title, was nicknamed by the miners 'Tommy Thunder', although not to his face.

Gasping and wheezing, Tommy arrived at Roundall's stint with his safety lamp hooked in a leather dog collar strapped around his neck.

This was the custom when the coalface was so low that the miners had to crawl along it on their knees. The collar ensured that the lamp hung vertically and thus stayed lit. He stopped near Roundall and squat on his haunches getting his breath back.

Between rasping breaths, with his finger and thumb he reached into his waistcoat pocket and extracted a pigtail screw of chewing tobacco. Placing the screw between his teeth he twisted the tobacco until a piece broke off and started chewing. It was known locally as 'Chomping on the chew'.

Despite being big and overweight, the miners at Redman's Colliery had a healthy respect for Tommy Thunder, as when he was in his twenties, he was one of the best boxing prizefighters around. On many occasions he would give the promoter of the boxing booth at Wigan's annual market fair a shock, when he floored his biggest, dirtiest and best booth fighter. He claimed the prize and lost the promoter a packet of money to the miners who had had side bets on Tommy.

In addition to the boxing reputation, the miners' fearful respect was compounded by the fact that Tommy had a good brain. He had attended Wigan and District Mining College for five years, three nights a week after a shift on the coalface, to gain his Second Class Undermanager's qualification.

This was no mean feat for a lad who'd left St Patrick's Catholic School at the age of twelve.

Tommy's trouble was that he had been in the mine so long that the pit had become the most important thing in his life. It came first, second and third, according to his wife,

Mabel.

The men had a nickname for this condition, which was 'pit burned', or as they pronounced it 'pit brunt' in Lancashire dialect.

'What time is it, Tommy?' enquired Roundall.

'Get on with thi work,' Tommy angrily angrily.

'Tommy, what time is it?' repeated Roundall.

'I've no watch,' lied Tommy.

'I can see thi watch-chain, on thi waistcoat,' Roundall retorted.

'It's broke! Get on with thi work,' Tommy balled.

'Tommy, for God's sake! Tell us what time it is.' roared Roundall, hardly believing that Tommy was being so pig-headed.

Tommy's face suddenly went bright-red, and from the corner of his mouth an angry hot spit of baccy juice flew out landing in the dust near Roundall's knee.

With enlarged eyes and staring directly into Roundall's, Tommy snatched the hunter pocketwatch from his waistcoat pocket, grabbed the watch with one hand and the chain with the other and snatched the two apart, breaking the chain. He then raised his right arm, and threw the watch fifty yards into the waste, where they both heard it smash into several pieces.

Tommy stared silently at Roundall for a few seconds. With large, glaring eyes he triumphantly bawled, 'Nay! Nobody knows bloody time. Get on with thi work.'

'You daft bugger,' said Roundall, shaking his head in disbelief, 'tha's pit brunt'.

Tommy left the coalface to finish his inspection rounds at the other coalfaces.

# *Two*

'Billy!' Edna shouted from the bottom of the stairs to her son. 'It's five o'clock. Come on, get up, it's Monday and your first day at pit. And go to lavvy, you won't have time later.'

Half asleep, Billy crawled out of bed, clumsily got dressed and went downstairs.

With half-closed eyes he sat at the table where his mother had laid out his Kellogg's cornflakes, a slice of toast, jam and a cup of tea. After eating his cereal, he bit into his toast and cried out, 'Mam! This bread's crap'. His mother gave Billy a sharp slap at the back of his head. 'Billy, don't talk like that in this house. It's a good job thi Dad's gone to pit early. It's good bread, fresh from Duva Bakery'.

'But Mam, you knows I only like Warburton's bread.'

'Get it down you,' replied his mother. 'Here's your water can and your snap tin. I've put your butties in it and added a piece of home-made cake. Hurry up, you know you can't be late on your first day.'

Billy was the only child of Edna and Johnny, and they lived in a small terraced house in one of many rows of pre-war terraced houses.

Billy left through the front door and, dragging his feet,

walked towards the bus stop to wait for the Wigan bus.

His mother stood at the front door with her arms folded watching her son amble on his way, wearing his flat cap and a scarf knitted by his Aunty Nelly. Her thoughts were sad as her 'poor little lad' set off to go down the pit. She wiped a tear from the corner of her eye.

'Eey up, Billy lad, art all reet,' greeted Brian Ellis, with a big grin on his face. Brian was another lad starting his first day at the same pit.

Billy and Brian had been at the same secondary modern school and they had left on the same day, both signing up with the National Coal Board.

'Ay Bry,' was Billy's cheerful response

'A mate a mine said there's a group that's absolutely brilliant, they play a really great new sound. They're calling it Rock and Roll. He told me that they've made a film called 'Rock around the Clock', and it's on at the Sems cimema next week, and all the girls stand up and dance. Fancy going?'

'Sounds great, Bry, let me know when it's on.'

'Ay, but first we have to get our first day at pit over, don't we.'

'Ay, but I wish I was still at school. Don't it seem strange, one day in a classroom and the next down pit.'

'Weird, but there's one thing though,' said Billy.

'What's that, Billy?'

'Well, we are no longer boys. At fifteen. We are now Men.'

They caught the five-thirty bus, which was already three-quarters full of men, travelling to the various pits in the Wigan area. Most were travelling upstairs where they could smoke, but as Billy and Brian didn't smoke, they boarded the bus and sat downstairs.

After walking down the country lane with other miners, they arrived at the pit.

It was six-fifteen when they rushed into the pithead baths. They had been warned by their trainer last week that there was no such thing as being late at a pit.

In common with all pits, precisely at six-fifty the cage stopped winding men, and the cages were converted to be able to load and carry full coal tubs up the shaft from the pit bottom, and empty ones down the shaft.

Anybody late missed what was called the last winding and was sent home with no pay.

Billy and Brian parted at the clean lockers as Brian's locker was at the other end of the building. Brian's first day was to be helping out in the joiners shop.

'Keep thi pecker up, pal' joked Brian, with a cheeky grin as he ran off.

'Chance would be a fine thing,' shouted Billy as he entered the baths building.

Billy found and opened his numbered locker and undressed, placing his clothes inside before moving to his dirty locker at the opposite side of the building, walking via the centrally located showers. He opened his dirty locker and got dressed in his nearly-new overalls, boots, belt and helmet the common issue to all new employees of the NCB.

Billy came from a family of miners, his dad having traced the direct family line back over the years. Billy was the seventh generation of miner in his family.

His grandad had joined up in 1914 and had survived the First World War. After his army discharge in 1919 he had returned to mining, only to be killed by a fall of stone on his second day down the pit.

Due to the fact that technically he was still an army

reserve, and as such still on the Army's books, he now lies buried in Wigan's Ince Cemetery where he had been given a war grave by the Army. His name, number and rank of gunner, along with the carved gun-carriage badge of the Royal Artillery was chiselled on the white marble headstone, although there was no reference to the way he died.

Billy, although never having met him, or even ever having seen a photo of him, was proud of this fine man. He would often stand in front of the gravestone thinking what a shame it was, him surviving the war when most of his mates were killed in the trenches, him surviving only to get flattened down the pit two days after being discharged.

Billy wondered what his grandad was like.


Billy joined the other miners as they left the baths. The men stopped near the exit to the baths to dab a thick blob of grease onto their boots or, in some cases with the older men, on their clogs, before using the revolving brushes which rubbed the grease into the leather of the footwear. Then they filled their water bottles at one of the many water taps.

Having done all this, as Billy was leaving one of his dad's drinking mates, Peter McKay, was leaving at the same time. Peter smiled and said, 'Hello, Billy. First day then?'

'Aye,' answered Billy.

'Welcome Billy. Come with me and I will show you the ropes and tell you what to do.'

They walked on to the lamp room where they obtained their battery-powered cap-lamps. Over each man's cap-lamp recharging station was a little hook on which hung a round brass tally bearing a stamp of the colliery name and the miner's individual number. The tally had to be handed to the man at the top of the shaft, who was called the banksman, before the men descended the shaft. This essential safety feature ensured that the colliery management knew exactly who was down the mine at any time.

At the end of a shift the miners collected their tallies, which had been sent down to the pit bottom later in the shift, and where they were placed on a numbered board near the pit bottom shaft, by young Jimmy Barlow, the cheeky pit bottom office clerk.

Some of the miners, in addition, to their cap-lamp, also collected a flame safety lamp. Ever since Sir Humphrey Davy invented the lamp in 1815, the lamp, consisting of a naked flame surrounded by a metal funnel mesh, had been keeping miners safe. He had discovered that when placed in an explosive mixture of methane and air, the gauze mesh would not allow the mixture to reach the safety lamp's flame and therefore the lamp wouldn't cause an explosion in the surrounding atmosphere.

When it was invented it was the only form of safe illumination in mines, but with the development of battery-powered cap-lamps its sole use changed to that of a safety agent for the testing of methane gas.

The flame safety lamp had been improved and developed over the years and a popular model in Lancashire and other mining areas was manufactured in Eccles. All the lamps carried an oval brass plate proudly displaying the company's name – 'Protector Lamp & Lighting Co.

It had long been known that when the flame was turned down to form a small bubble of blue flame over the wick, if any gas was present in the surrounding area, a faint, ghostly white triangle formed on top of the flame and was clearly visible. If the triangle formed an equilateral triangle shape then the percentage mixture of gas was about two and a half per cent. As a mixture of methane and air becomes explosive at between five and fifteen per cent the Coal Mines Act stipulated that two and a half per cent was the limit for coal producing working and at that point all electrical equipment in the area was required to be turned off. Therefore the officials – the Undermanager, Deputy and the shot-firers were trained in the testing procedures and had to test for gas at regular intervals. They had also to prove their competence by taking a gas test every three years.

Officials were easily recognised by their more distinctive safety lamps, as the top half of their safety lamps, called the bonnet, was manufactured from shiny chrome metal. In addition, their lamp also included a mechanism whereby the lamp, if extinguished, could be relit by the use of a built-in ratchet pin, which when pulled out and hit sharply caused a spark near to the wick to relight the lamp. Ordinary miners' safety lamps had a dull-black metal bonnet and no re-lighting pin.


The men carried on towards the shaft and ascended three flights of wide wooden stairs to the pit head. Here they were stopped by a deputy who had been allocated the duty of checking all who were going underground.

The procedure consisted of him first checking the miners' flame safety lamp, which he did by twisting the base, to see that it was properly locked and then, holding each flame safety lamp at eye level, taking a deep breath and blowing at the glass, whilst watching the flame to see for any flicker. A flicker meant that the glass was not sealed properly and if unsealed or unlocked, the miner had to return back to the lamp room for a replacement. Having passed this test, the men were then frisked by the deputy as he searched them for matches, lighters or cigarettes. A large sign behind him declared in large red letters, 'WARNING NO CONTRABAND'. After being searched, the miners stood waiting for their turn to enter the cage and descend the shaft.

Billy stood watching as a deputy who was ready to go down the mine walked over to a tall, narrow, wooden box that was fastened to the wall near to the mineshaft. It housed an aneroid barometer. The deputy tapped the glass of the barometer gently with his bony knuckle and adjusted a brass-knurled screw so that its small vernier scale was positioned at the top of the column of mercury.

'Peter?' said Billy. 'What's that deputy doing?'

'Well, Billy, a barometer, as you probably know from school science, measures the atmospheric pressure. You see that sign over there?' he said as he pointed to a large, red sign located over the barometer.

Billy looked up to see the sign, which read, 'BEWARE FALLING BAROMETER'.

'That's a daft sign. Why don't they just screw the barometer on properly, then it won't fall?'

Peter burst out laughing.

'No, Billy, what it means is, when the atmospheric pressure is falling. Every mine is warned of this by the meterological office. Then that red light above the sign is switched on, to warn the deputies.'

'Why do they need to know that?' enquired Billy.

'Well, Billy, as the coalface moves forward, the area where the coal has been taken by the previous shift is left open and unsupported. This area is called 'the waste' and it is unventilated. Eventually it becomes full of methane gas. Now normally this is okay, as the barometric pressure in the atmosphere holds it back. However, if the barometric pressure falls, then some of the gas expands and escapes onto the working face and this presents a danger to the men on the coalface. The deputies, on seeing the red sign lit up, become more vigilant in their testing for gas.'

'Aye,' retorted the deputy searching the men, who had overheard Peter's lecture. 'If you remember your science lessons from school, lad, it obeys Boyles law — if the pressure falls, the volume expands.'

'Wow,' exclaimed Billy.


The men stood in a silent group at the top of the shaft. The cage rose suddenly from the shaft, held in the grip of a giant chain claw.

When the cage stopped level with the landing where the men were standing, the banksman controlling the loading of the miners pulled a lever which pushed large, steel wedge-shaped stops, known locally as 'keps' under the cage. This was a secondary precaution to prevent the cage from moving down the shaft whilst the men were entering it. The banksman then lifted the cage gate, and the first thirty men handed their tallyies to him, as they stooped to enter the cage.

Young Billy and Peter were amongst the first thirty. The banksman dropped the gate, which made a loud crashing noise making Billy jump.

He then pulled the lever to remove the keps from under the cage and tapped the bell signal button five times, which caused a ringing echo around the pithead.

The signal was relayed to the winding engine-house, to tell the winding engineer that men were descending, and to start the winding motor to slowly lower the cage into the bowels of the earth.

In the cage it was silent and it suddenly went jet black. The men, all squashed together, had turned their cap-lamps off, and as was normal, had casually slung the lamp cable around their necks.This made Billy think that they looked like strange doctors wearing stethoscopes.

Suddenly the cage dropped rapidly, catching Billy unaware. He held his breath and suppressed a cry, gulping nervously.

One of the men switched his cap-lamp on, instantly dazzling everyone in the cage with the sudden glare of its bright light.

'Switch that off, you silly sod,' cursed one of the Halliwell twins, angrily. In mining terms the Halliwell twins, tunnellers, were each built like a 'brick shit house'. The guilty man went quiet and quickly turned off his lamp.

After a descent of nine hundred and fifty yards the cage came to an abrupt halt. The man at the pit bottom, who was called the 'onsetter', raised the safety gate and the men exited the cage into a large, well-lit tunnel roadway. It was laid with rails and two lines of both full, and empty, metal tubs.

Peter McKay pointed to a man a few yards away and said 'Billy, report to Charlie Wood over there; he's the Pit Bottom Deputy and will be your boss for the next few weeks.'

'Thanks, Peter, see you later.'

# *Three*

The canteen was a large, square, flat-roofed brick building half-way between the lamp room and the steps to the pit headgear. It was spotlessly clean, mainly due to the efforts of Ivy, the manageress, who supervised with a rod of iron, and her four assistants. There was also an area set aside for miners on their way to, and after coming up from, the pit in their dirty clothes.

It was said that here, at Redman's canteen, you could buy the best pies in Lancashire, made on the premises by the canteen ladies. Also on the menu, three days a week, was a favourite of the men — pea soup. This was a mass of dense green-pea soup, cooked in a large cauldron, to which was added several whole pigs' feet. These pigs' feet eventually broke up during the cooking process to release their meat and form a thick jelly which gave the soup its flavour and body. Most of the men were unaware that the meat was pigs' feet, but the majority probably wouldn't have been bothered anyway.

Ivy, a large, round woman, had been in charge of the canteen for many years. She had raised seven children and four of her sons now worked at Redman's colliery. She had short, permed hair, a ruddy face and a jolly outlook on life, but she took pride in her canteen and was proud of its products and her team.

Ivy stood, this Monday morning, with her hands on her hips, watching Jenny, one of her ladies, laying the freshly-baked meat pies out to cool on racks. They released a delicious aroma which pervaded the canteen.

Following in Jenny's wake was Peggy, who held a steel jug containing hot water, to which had been added gelatine. It was Peggy's job to add this mixture to each individual pie. When cold, the liquid would set to a solid jelly. When the pies were later warmed in the oven, this jelly would once again become a rich, runny liquid, which the men would suck out, sometimes loudly, before it trickled down their arm.

'No! No!,' barked Ivy.

'Peggy, how many times do I have to tell you, don't use your finger to make a hole in the pies for the jelly; use the end of a wooden spoon.

God, if Environmental Health came in and saw you, we would all be in big trouble.'

'Sorry, I wasn't thinking,' said Peggy rather sheepishly, as she grabbed a wooden spoon which she then used to make a hole in the pie and continued her job of pouring the jelly mixture into each pie.

At the other end of the kitchen Nellie, at twenty-six the youngest of the ladies in the canteen, was stirring the cauldron of pea soup with a large ladle.

'Mug of tea, love,' ordered Nobby, a surface worker, to Sheila, the fifth lady of the canteen team. It was her turn today to be on counter duty. Sheila walked over to the urn and pressed the tap to fill the mug with hot steaming tea.

'Milk and sugar, Nobby?' Sheila asked.

'Aye, milk and two sugars, please love,' replied Nobby.

Sheila added a splash of sterilised milk from a bottle on the counter, and added two sugars from a basin alongside.

'Oh, and I'll have a Chorley Cake while you're at it, and don't try to fob me off with an Eccles Cake like you did last time. There's a world of difference, you know, besides being made in different towns,' said Nobby, cheekily.

'They're all the same to me,' quipped Sheila, as she placed a Chorley Cake on a plate in front of Nobby.

'Well your taste buds must have dropped out when you had all your teeth out,' the surface worker joked

'Cheeky bugger,' rebuked Sheila. 'I've got all me own teeth.'

After paying Nobby sat down with a grin on his face and winked at Sheila. She glared back at him, but as she turned away she secretly smiled to herself at his cheek.

It was lunchtime for some of the surface workers and Nobby was soon joined at his table by a group of others, grasping their mugs of tea and lunch boxes. As they opened their food boxes and began to eat, Nobby, being the surface joker, addressed them with, 'Have you heard the story about lucky Raymond and last Friday's draw in here?' He secretly winked at his best mate, Mark.

'Well,' he continued, 'Raymond, the lamp room attendant, has bought a raffle ticket from this canteen every Friday, without fail, for ten years and never won.'

'As he was retiring last Friday, the welfare committee got together and, feeling sorry him, decided to fix it so that Raymond would win the big prize of £100 on the day he retired.'

'To ensure that he won they put into the hat raffle tickets that all had the same number. Ivy was to ensure that when Raymond bought his ticket it would be the one with this number. All the committee men agreed, and were in on the

17

act.'

'So, Friday came and the canteen was packed. Everybody was excited and chattering away.'

Nobby stopped talking and took a quick sip of his tea before animately continuing.

'"Quiet, everyone," cried the Chairman, standing on a chair. "It's Friday draw time and I would just like to say today is Raymond's last day here at Redman's, so as a special honour we are going to ask him to draw the winning ticket from the hat."'

'All the men smiled, and nudged each other, one muttering, "Lucky Raymond, drawing his own ticket. Watch his face."'

'So the chairman held the hat up high and Raymond stood up on a chair to reach into the hat.'

'As Raymond pulled one from the hat, the chairman shouted, "Now, Raymond, read out the winning number."'

'Raymond, to a stunned silence, looked down with a puzzled expression on his face.'

'"Come on, Raymond, read it out," shouted someone.'

'Raymond opened his mouth and in a clear, loud voice said, "Six and seven eighths."'

Nobby stopped speaking and there was a few seconds' silence in the canteen, before the men burst out laughing at Nobby's story.

One bloke in the group looked puzzled. 'I don't get it!' he confessed, which made the men laugh even more.

'You daft sod,' said Nobby. 'He drew out the hat size. Lucky Raymond?'

The hooter then went to signal that break time was over and the men left the canteen still chuckling as they went back to their work.

'Did you hear that,' joked Ivy to the other women, who were still laughing, 'that tale will go down in Redman's history as a true story.'

# *Four*

Frank Taylor was a young, ambitious lad who had his sights on becoming a colliery manager, which in any mining town in Great Britain is the equivalent of God.

Frank was brought up in the mining community and had learned from being a lad that any true-blooded Lancashire mining son had the pit in his blood.

Frank was different, in that although he could see his deep, inbred loyalties in the pit, the comradeship and faithfulness to mates, he felt that there had to be something more to the life.

Frank realised this when he passed his eleven plus exam at the first attempt.

So, after Grammar School he signed on at the Wigan Mining College.

The coursework came easy to Frank and he soon took the lead within the class and after six years was awarded The City and Guilds of London first prize Silver Medal for mining.

He was now enrolled on what was called a sandwich course, so-named because he had to attend college for six months and then spend the next six months at a colliery to gain practical mining experience.

For his six months' practical he had been directed to Redman's Colliery and found life here completely different.

Here there was no spoon-fed lifestyle, and respect had to be earned.

Frank reported for his first day at the colliery in a state of slight nervous anticipation. He had been told to introduce himself to the Chief Administration officer at Redman's Colliery, Mr Robert Kilpatrick.


Now Mr Kilpatrick was not, in the true sense, a traditional mining man. He was, in fact, what was known at the time as a Bevin Boy, named after the Government's Minister of Labour, Ernest Bevin, who'd come up with a solution to the growing coal crisis.

The indiscriminate conscription of working coal miners to the armed forces had brought about a shortage of much-needed coal production. At first it seemed easy: miners would not be called-up for the forces and men could volunteer to go down the mines. However this measure did not produce enough miners, so Bevin directed that every fifth man registered would be directed to the mines instead of the armed forces and these men became known as Bevin Boys.

Mr Robert Kilpatrick was something of a toff, brought up in a wealthy family who had made their fortune from coffee in Kenya in the early nineteen hundreds, but who were now merchant bankers in the City.

Robert had been sent off to the same private school as his father and grandfather had attended, thus maintaining the family tradition.

The fact that he had been allocated as a Bevin Boy was a great shock to Robert and his family, as he was all set to go to Edinburgh University to study medicine. The family had tried to use their powerful financial and political influence to overturn the decision, but to no avail.

Reluctantly, Robert had started at Redman's Colliery. The blow, however, was softened by his family being acquainted with the Colliery Manager, Mr W R Sankey. After his initial training, Mr Sankey had appointed Robert to the position of Colliery Administration Officer.

Much to Robert's surprise, he took to the job and threw himself into the work with enthusiasm. He saw that administration at the colliery ran as smoothly as the pithead winding gear.

Robert Kilpatrick had now been in the position for fifteen years, even though he could have left by now. His family tried in vain to persuade him to recommence his medical studies or take up a position in the family banking business. To their disappointment he had refused, informing them that he was really happy in his work at Redman's Colliery.

Over the years the Area management had also come to realise Robert's true value, and they encouraged him to develop his skills. He had taken accounting exams, which he found quite easy, and had become a fully qualified Chartered Accountant, after which he had been promoted to Chief Administrative Officer.

Mr Sankey, the Colliery Manager, knew Robert's worth and felt fortunate to have such a talented officer working for him. Over the years they had become firm friends, with a mutual respect for each other.

Mr Kilpatrick signed up Frank Taylor as a young trainee Manager and gave him the task of reviewing the deputies' pre-shift safety inspection reports.

After about four months, because Frank was a friendly

and outgoing lad, he became very popular with the men both underground and on the surface. When he was on surface duties one of his favourite places to visit was the blacksmiths' shop, to chat to the blacksmiths as they worked forging metal. In fact, every day when he was on surface duties Frank would contrive to have his morning brew with the blacksmiths, who on the signal of the pit whistle, would down their tools and gather in the centre of the blacksmiths' shop with their hot drinks.

This is where one day, Frank heard a fascinating story about a young lad at a neighbouring pit trying to drag a cat across the canal.

He wondered, after hearing the tale, if the blacksmiths were actually pulling his leg.

# *Five*

The blacksmiths' shop was a large, oblong, well-lit building. Along one wall, at regular intervals, were four forges which held roaring coke fires. In front of each one sat a large black anvil plus a water tank for the rapid cooling of hot metal.

Frank Taylor loved the smells and the warmth of the building, especially in winter; he loved the noise and the humour and interests of the men working here.

Today, Frank was on surface duties and he had arrived at the shop just as the whistle blew to indicate it was brew time.

He sat with the men, in a circle in the centre of the shop, as each sipped their mug of tea.

Albert was one of the blacksmith's assistants. He had the job of holding the pieces of hot metal with forging tongs,whilst the blacksmith struck decisive and accurate blows to the metal, shaping it to form the work. In addition, he also had to bring and fetch supplies for the blacksmiths. Albert was totally unaware that when talking he often made malapropisms in his statements, much to the delight of the blacksmiths. Unbeknown to Albert the men kept a secret list of his utterings and added to it regular updates.

Some of his prized sayings recorded on the list were:

'Labour had a lot of electrical votes'

'Eeh, my nose is sore. I think I've got a pallias up it!'

'We have plenty of hot water at our house now we have had an electric emergency heater fitted!'

And what was considered a classic:

'Wife works at a material factory in Bolton, and the other day came home from the factory shop with a Rembrandt for only ten bob'.


Dan, the Foreman Blacksmith, was considered by his men, and indeed most of Redman Colliery, to be a wise and clever man.

Dan had years of experience in the job, having started as a young apprentice blacksmith and worked his way up to be a foreman.

He was a devout Methodist, worshipping every Sunday, and was a Senior Trustee at the local Methodist Church.

He did not swear but could give his men a good tongue-lashing without using a single swear word.

Although his men feared Dan they had a great respect for him, his only vice being his love of full-strength cigarettes.

As Frank sat down with the men, Dan remarked, 'Hello, Frank. I was just telling this lot,' taking a sip from his tin mug, and taking a drag on his cigarette, 'my mate Ronnie, the Foreman Blacksmith at Bickershaw Colliery, was relating a story the other day, about how it was impossible to drag a cat across the canal, which he assured me is a true tale, as it had actually happened again last July.'

'The Bickershaw blacksmiths would wait until a new young lad who had newly started at the pit, was present —

someone a bit like young Tommy here.'

'Oh aye, a bit gullible, dust tha' mean, Dan?' laughed Albert.

'Shut up, Albert. Go on, Dan, carry on,' rebuked Freddy the senior blacksmith.

Dan continued with his mate's story.

'Ronnie told me this is what happened. All Ronnie's men knew what was coming, when one morning's tea break Ronnie said casually that he had heard that it is impossible to drag a cat across a canal, as when a cat sees water, you cannot move it for love nor money.'

'Another blacksmith present would say that was rubbish, and a great debate would follow, ending on suggestions for how they could test the theory.'

'It was decided that the best way would be to take a rope and throw it across the canal.'

'Then, very carefully, someone on the other bank would fasten a cat by its collar onto the rope, the man at the other end would then take up the slack. The cat would be placed about a foot away from the canal bank, then when the cat saw the water, it would dig its claws into the bank and they would then see if the bloke at the other side could pull the cat in.'

'The doubter would then make the point that if they did it they would need a volunteer to be at the other end of the rope to pull the cat in, and they would want someone impartial.'

'At this stage the new lad, in this case an apprentice blacksmith called Norman, a well-known and likeable young lad from the village, could not contain his enthusiasm. He began to beg them to let him be the one to try it. At first, they ignored him, they then very reluctantly agreed that he would be ideal.

'It was agreed to arrange the event for the second Saturday in July.

Word soon spread around the pit, both on the surface and underground, that young Norman was going to attempt to drag a cat across the canal.'

Arguments raged with the general consensus of opinion being that it would be a piece-of-cake for the young lad to drag the cat into the water.'

'On the Friday, at eleven o' clock, the day before the event, the blacksmiths had made sure that everything was ready for the following morning.'

'They later learned from Norman that he had awoken early on the Saturday in question, and as he was dressing had thought it all too easy. He had also reflected on how all that week men underground and on the surface had encouraged him, congratulating him on his efforts. He had felt that, at least now he was something of a celebrity, as most of the pit had said they were going to attend. Even Captain Stead the Area General manager had promised to call and watch.'

'On the day itself, at the Colliery, which is adjacent to the canal, a group of the blacksmiths had earlier set off for the canal armed with a rope, the fitters' shop cat, and a cat's collar.'

'At about ten-fifty-five both banks of the canal were crowded with men, their wives and even in some cases their children, who passed the time skimming flat stones across the water to see how many times they could get them to bounce across to the other side.'

'Norman had arrived at the pit side of the canal bank as instructed, and was met by two of the blacksmiths.'

'One had encouraged Norman. "All right, lad, don't be nervous. I know there's a big crowd, but they are all behind thee".'

'Ronnie, at the other side of the canal threw a weight across, attached to which was a clothesline. One of the blacksmiths had caught the line and pulled it across. Ronnie had then attached to the clothesline a heavy hemp rope, which was then pulled across.'

'When he had got the heavy hemp rope, he had untied the clothes line and had commanded, "Come on, lad, over here." Norman had then jogged across to the rope. He then instructed Norman, "Listen, lad, when you start to pull, there is a good chance that cat will go mad, and snatch this rope fast, so it could burn thi hands, then tha'll let go, and have lost. What I'm suggesting is that we tie this rope around your waist, then if you have to let go, all is not lost. Okay, Norman?" "Brilliant,"replied Norman. "Let's do it".'

'So the blacksmith, being a fisherman, had expertly tied a clove hitch in the rope around Norman's waist. At the other side, Ronnie had tied the rope to the collar of Tabby, the Fitting shop's Tomcat.'

'"Ready!' balled Albert.'

'A loud cheer went out from the crowd.'

'"Take up the slack Norman," he shouted.'

'Norman had spit on his hands and made a few scuffmarks in the pit waste surface of the canal bank and replied, "Ready".'

'Norman was totally unaware of the fact that the whole event was a big joke, which most of the crowd were a party to, due to having heard the story from their parents.'

'Word had spread like wildfire throughout the pit that a practical joke was to be played on young Norman, and everyone had played their part.

As Norman had taken up the slack he could see, at the other side, in a gap in the crowd, Tabby the cat with the thick hemp rope tied to his collar. However, what Norman could not see, was that the rope continued out of sight down the opposite embankment, where three large blacksmiths were holding it firmly, with big grins fixed on their faces.'

'When the rope was reasonably tight, Ronnie yelled "Pull" and Norman started to pull on the rope, his face deadly serious."

'He had looked puzzled as the cat had not appeared to move, but began digging in at his pull.'

'He had then felt the rope, very minutely, pull him towards the canal ... and immediately, he knew!'

'The crowd, watching his face intently, let out a bawling laugh, and went wild with delight when they saw realisation dawn on his face.'

'"Shit!" he had thought. "I am a stupid bugger," as inch by inch he went nearer to the water.'

'It had been no use struggling, as the rope was tied around his waist. There was no escape. With a mighty splash, Norman fell into the canal to a great cheer from the crowd. Spluttering, he had swum to the opposite canal bank and had climbed out of the water to a great cheer.'

'Standing on the canal bank with a big smile on his face he had turned to the crowd, wiped his face and bowed, as they clapped with delight at his dignified acceptance.'

'The blacksmiths gathered around him patting him on the back saying, "Well done, lad, but thy's not first one to be fooled. Captain Stead was the last one when he was a trainee many years ago."'

'Later, in the blacksmiths' workshop, when Norman had showered and changed, the assembled blacksmiths had presented Norman with a certificate to commemorate the event and £50 cash, which had been collected from the crowd, as a thank you for that morning's entertainment.'

Dan's staff all thought that this was a great story, that would go down in Leigh folk law history.

Frank returned to his duties laughing and shaking his head in amazement, wondering if the story was really true.

# Six

The local mines rescue station was located at the nearby village of Westbury. Here, three teams of full-time rescue men were employed. Each team consisted of ten men working eight-hour shifts to ensure that there was always a full team in the station twenty-four hours a day in case an emergency situation occurred in one of the mines in the area.

These full-time rescue men were supplemented by part-time rescuers, who were regular miners at the local pits, and who had volunteered and been trained by the rescue service.

In an emergency at their pit, these part-time rescue team members would leave their regular jobs and team up with the full-time brigade. At Redman's Colliery, Roundall and Tommy Green, the Undermanager, were both trained part-time rescuers.

The training was very intensive and the service only recruited fit and healthy miners. They had to undergo the vigorous 'Harvard Pack Test,' which each one of them had to pass to prove his fitness before he could be a member of the team. As the name suggests, this test was originally designed at America's Harvard University, to test athletes.

This meant that each rescue member had to have a third of his body weight strapped to his back, and at one second intervals step up and down on a step sixteen inches high, for five minutes.

To ensure that the rescue men kept up to date with mining developments, and also remain fit, regular mock exercises were arranged at local pits.

This Wednesday an exercise had been arranged at Redman's Colliery, but only for the full-time rescuers. At the colliery, the Ventilation Officer, Ged Winstanley, had the job of designing new scenarios and arranging the exercise details. Ged's normal job, as a senior official at the pit, was to ensure that the mine had sufficient ventilation to keep the mine free from any dangerous or harmful gasses.

He had a team who regularly went underground and measured the flow of air in all the roadways using an instrument called an anemometer; in addition they had to take weekly air samples at every coalface, which were sent to the NCB's area laboratory for full analysis of the air's gasses. These measurements were required under the Coal Mines Regulations, which had to be strictly followed. These routine measures were in addition to the regular checks and tests, made by the colliery deputies, for gas using their flame safety lamps, ensuring that the mine maintained a safe environment.

For this exercise Ged had decided that the scenario would be that an explosion had started a fire in an old district that was no longer worked.

The team would be required to build a sandbag wall called a 'stopping' across the roadway, which would then completely cut off the ventilation supply to the area, thus extinguishing the imaginary fire. To give the exercise some reality, Ged would fill the tunnel with dense artifical smoke, thus requiring the rescuers to wear breathing apparatus, a somewhat arduous task.

On the day of the exercise the team arrived at the colliery in their distinctive bright blue vans. After testing their oxygen cylinders they descended the mine along with Ged, who was carrying one of Redman's faithful canaries.

The canary's role in the mine was to show if any carbon monoxide was present in the mine atmosphere. Carbon monoxide was rarely found, thankfully, as it is a deadly gas having no smell or taste but which can kill in very small amounts. The body's blood has a great affinity for carbon monoxide and the blood will absorb it in preference to oxygen, until the blood saturation reaches such a level that it causes the body to go into a deep unconscious state, never to wake up, the state being called carboxyhemoglobin.

The canary, having a more delicate respiratory system, was used as its blood supply and lungs reacted much sooner than humans. When the canary fell from its perch the miners had enough time to escape the area before they became affected.

Many miners kept pigeons at home, which were housed in brightly-painted sheds with colourful vertical stripes. Their birds were entered into local and national pigeon championships and keeping them was a serious and popular hobby, , with star birds having a high monetary value.

It was said, proudly by the miners, that the Queen herself was a pigeon fancier and had a large flock of birds, and she even had appointed a Royal pigeon keeper.

Miners therefore loved and respected the tiny, yellow life-saving canary and were happy in the knowledge that when the little bird fell to the gas it would be revived immediately with a miniature oxygen cylinder, especially designed into the bird's cage.

As the rescue party arrived in the exercise area, a man who had been pre-briefed came running towards them shouting, 'There's been an explosion and a fire is blazing back there.'

The rescue team began to prepare their breathing apparatus charged with liquid oxygen.

As they left the pit bottom Ged handed over the canary to the team captain, as Ged was staying behind at the pit bottom.

They entered the tunnel which had now filled with dense smoke. The beams of their lamps hardly made any impression on the smoke.

They walked swiftly along the roadway, carrying an empty stretcher along with their fist-aid kit and resuscitation equipment.

As the area was very old the roadway at one point became very low, so the rescue men had to crawl along and drag their equipment behind them. Arriving at the exercise area they carried out a detailed search for casualties. After finding none they assembled at the area where Ged had arranged for a stock of sandbags to be stored.

The Captain, using a system of signals with his rubber-bulb hooter, appropriate gestures and written notes on message pads, started to direct the men to start building a sandbag wall across the roadway. They soon had the stopping wall a quarter of the way up the roadway area when the Captain ordered the men to stop working.

At this stage the heat and humidity had increased, due to the wall having reduced the available airflow. This presented the danger that the hot humid conditions could cause the men to collapse, through heat stroke. He took a number of readings of the relative humidity using an instrument called a 'hygrometer', which resembled a football rattle as he whirled it around to take the reading.

Having established that the humidity was acceptable, he looked across to see the canary happily chirping away. He tested the air for methane and, being satisfied with the conditions, indicated for the men to continue with the stopping.

After about an hour the stopping was complete. They had built into the stopping wall a steel three-inch pipe which ran through the wall. Attached to this, at the face end, was a quarter-inch brass nipple, which would allow Ged's team to take regular air samples from behind the stopping to know the state of the atmosphere in the old workings.

The Captain then instructed the team to gather up all their equipment and proceed to the pit bottom.

At the pit bottom the men met up with Ged. As they entered the fresh air they removed their equipment. Ged could see that all of them were sweating heavily.

'Alright, lads, I bet you've lost a few pounds today, eh?'

'Aye, Ged' laughed one of the men as he handed the canary back to Ged. 'Get us up that shaft quick. I'm dying for a drink, a cig and some of Ivy's pea soup.'

So the men entered the cage and ascended to the surface. They entered the canteen still with their breathing apparatus strapped to their back, as they were so hungry they couldn't wait until they got changed.

On walking in they were met with:'Oh, my goodness! Look ladies. Martians have just landed,' from Ivy.

As the men lined up for their pea soup at the canteen counter, Nellie, who had an eye on one of the tall handsome rescue men, nudged Jenny out of the way.'Move, Jenny, I'll serve these brave handsome men.'

The men all burst out laughing when they followed

Nellie's eyes to the lad who was the youngest of the team.

The manager was later informed that another successful exercise had taken place and that he had gained a free stopping.

# *Seven*

The telephone rang in the colliery manager's office at Redman's Colliery, and Robert Kilpatrick picked up the phone

'Good morning, Robert Kilpatrick here. How may I help you?'

'Oh hello, Mr Kilpatrick. This is Elizabeth Hardy from the National Coal Board Headquarters in Hobart House, London. I've been asked by the Deputy Coal Board Chairman to ring you about a proposed visit by Government VIPs. Your colliery has been selected.'

'Right, Miss Hardy, I presume it is Miss?'

'Yes,' she replied in a cheerful voice, 'and please call me Elizabeth.'

'Oh, okay, Elizabeth.' Robert sensed that Elizabeth was flirting with him, which to his surprise he found he quite enjoyed. He continued, 'I am the Chief Administrative Officer for the colliery and, it's Robert, by the way. I'll inform Mr Sankey, the Manager, but first can you give me some more details, such as when, who will be visiting, and why Redman's?'

'Well, Robert, I am the head of the Public Relations

section of Hobart House, and it seems that the new Government has been receiving a lot of criticism lately, since they announced that future power generating stations will mainly be fired by gas and oil, and in the near future nuclear power. The Prime Minister is keen to show to the media and public alike that he has not forgotten the coal industry. Hence the visit, which he will also be attending. During the visit he intends to give a speech to the media on the future role of coal in the United Kingdom.'

'Fine, Elizabeth, but why Redman's?'

'Well, Robert, your colliery location is right in the middle of the Lancashire coalfield. I feel it suits the Tory government perfectly, as rumour has it that the Prime Minister may soon call a general election, and most towns in your area are represented by Labour MPs. Consequently he wants the visit to be within the next two weeks, and has suggested Tuesday the nineteenth. Selected members of the cabinet will be joining the Prime Minister on the visit. Unfortunately, due to the short notice, the Coal Board Chairman, who is on a fact-finding tour of Germany, looking into coalface mechanisation, will be unable to attend. He has ordered his deputy, Sir Alf Kenyon, to attend in his place, and he has delegated me to sort out the details.'

'Right, Elizabeth, I think I have enough information for the moment. Can you fax me the schedule, timing and numbers at your earliest convenience please?'

'Will do, Robert, and I must say it is good to speak to someone who seems calm and organised. I can tell you this unexpected visit is causing chaos here. Yes, I will fax further details later. Goodbye, Robert.'

'Goodbye, Elizabeth, and thank you for the kind words.' Robert put down the telephone with a broad grin on his face.

Robert knocked politely on the Manager's adjoining door and walked in.

The room had a large picture window opposite the door, with a view of the Redman's Colliery headgear.

At the moment Robert could see the pulley wheel revolving quickly — an indication that coal was being wound. He knew from the past that when the manager observed the wheel was stopped for more than fifteen minutes, he would immediately be on the phone to the underground demanding to know what the delay was.

The Manager, Bill Sankey, was a very experienced colliery manager, having previously been the Manager of Snibston Colliery, in the aptly-named East Midlands town of Coalville. He had also spent a number of years working at Parkhouse Colliery in Clay Cross, Derbyshire.

As befitted his station, Bill Sankey sat at a large, oak, leather-topped desk, on the surfaces of which were several telephones and a number of reports that he was busily going through. Neatly stacked on a shelf to his right were several mining text books, next to which sat a mahogany-framed barograph, its chart showing a blue wavy line indicating the week's barometric pressure.

Mounted on the adjacent wall was a collection of Heath Robinson cartoon prints, depicting humorous mining scenes, alongside of which was Bill Sankey's framed First Class Mines Certificate.

Earlier in that week, the colliery manager, along with his undermanager Tommy Green, had been carrying out a safety inspection of some old underground workings that had ceased production some forty years ago, when a large stone had fallen on the manager's foot. With Tommy's help he had managed to hobble out of the area and be helped to the surface. Unfortunately, he had fractured his ankle, which was now encased in a plastercast. Determined to carry on working, with the aid of a walking stick, he would limp around the colliery, keeping his beady eye on the operations of his workforce.

He looked up, 'Robert, some of these Deputy's reports just don't make sense. I must have a word with young Tommy. Now, what can I do for you?'

'Bill, you won't believe the call I've just had. I've just had a telephone call from Hobart House.' Robert gave the manager the details he had received from Miss Hardy.

'Damm it! what next, what a turn-up. Me with a broken ankle, just when we are back in profit for the last six months, we get this bombshell thrown at us! I suspect that politics are involved here. We must try to work it to our advantage and try to influence the Prime Minister on the positive aspect of coal for the good of his balance of payments policy.

Now, Robert, what to do? Obviously I need all the details as soon as possible. Sit down, let's have a quick brainstorming session.'

Robert sat down and Bill continued, 'Do you think it would be a good idea if you went down to London to get more information?'

'Yes, I do, if you can spare me.' He then suggested he also arrange a meeting with Sir Alf Kenyon, and possibly someone from the government.

Bill thought that was a good idea, as he knew Sir Alf to be a good straight-talking person who might have more thoughts on the visit.

'Right then, get your train ticket booked and then let's draw up an action plan. Now, Robert, let's make a start here, get a team together in the conference room this afternoon. I want my pit to be perfect for the nineteenth. Contact Tommy and get him to come up the pit for the meeting and I also want Frank Taylor, and all the surface foremen and make sure your Admin staff are available to take notes.'

'Don't forget Ivy from the canteen and anyone else you feel should be included.'

'Okay, Bill. I'll draw up an attendance list and I'll let them all know right away.'

He returned to his office to think about who would be needed at the meeting. He booked an early train for the next day after contacting the various people and arranging the meeting. He rang Elizabeth Hardy at Hobart House.

'Hello, Elizabeth', he said, when she answered. 'There has been a development at my end.'

'Oh hello, Robert. Good to hear your voice again. What's that?'

'Well, my Manager, Bill Sankey, wants me to travel to London in the morning and visit Hobart House to get the details in person.'

'OK, Robert, that's a surprise. What do you want me to arrange?'

'Could you please try to arrange an appointment for me to see the Deputy Chairman, Sir Alf Kenyon, if possible tomorrow morning? My train is scheduled to arrive at Euston station at ten minutes past nine. I'm sorry to burden you with all this work, Elizabeth, but could you also contact the Prime Minister's Office for me to consult with the Secretary responsible for making the arrangements for the visit? Also, I will need a list of the people on the visit, their titles, the timing schedule and any other information that you could provide. Phew!'

'No problem, Robert. Leave all that to me. I've been taking notes whilst you have been talking. I will let you know what I have been able to arrange and, Robert, I will

41

meet your train at Euston. I will be waiting under the station clock, and have transport waiting to take us back to Hobart House. I look forward to meeting you tomorrow. Goodbye Robert.'

'Goodbye ,Elizabeth.'

Elizabeth Hardy replaced the telephone and thought that Robert Kilpatrick sounded rather nice, but she wondered what he was really like.

Little did she know that Robert Kilpatrick, Chief Administrative Officer, was at that moment thinking exactly the same thing.


The meeting assembled at two o'clock in the conference room, and all the invitees sat around a long table with the colliery manager at its head.

Addressing the meeting the manager said, 'Right, everyone, as you have just heard from Mr Kilpatrick, the VIP visit is to take place on Tuesday the nineteenth of July, and the Prime Minister himself will be included in the party.' A buzz of muttered conversation went around the room.

'Mr Kilpatrick is travelling down to London tomorrow to get the final details. I want this colliery to gleam; anything looking tatty I want it replacing.'

Looking directly at the foreman painter he then said, 'Anything that doesn't move, get your men to paint it white. Also whitewash the stones at the colliery entrance. We want to give a good impression. I want the stores to make sure they have a sufficient quantity of brand new protective clothing — helmets, overalls, boots and belts and cap-lamp batteries for our visitors. Also I want every workman, both surface and underground, issued with a brand new pair of safety gloves. Ivy, what can you do in the way of canapés?'

'What's canapés, Mr Sankey?'

'Tit bits to you, Ivy,' he chuckled. 'Can you fix it?'

'Yes, Mr Sankey, but seeing they are from London do you think I should make some Chelsea buns?'

Laughing, Bill replied 'No, Ivy no need to go so far.'

'Okay, no problem, Mr Sankey, but what about proper food when they come up pit? Do you want pies?'

'No, Ivy, what I want you to do is set up a buffet here in the conference room at the right time .Can you cope with that, or do you want me to get caterers in?'

'God forbid, Mr Sankey. Me and my girls can cope. In fact we will look forward to it, we will do you proud you'll see.'

Turning to the baths superintendent he said, 'Make sure that the visitors' changing rooms are spick-and-span and that the showers are in good working order.'

'How will they get here, Mr Sankey?' enquired Frank Taylor.

'They will be travelling first class on the train. We will need to arrange that a small executive coach or cars meets them at the station, and conveys them to Redman's. Can you arrange that please?' he said, pointing to the Area Transport Manager.

'Leave that to me, Mr Sankey,' he responded.

'I want to make the rescue room available as a media centre. Can someone make sure that it has extra desks and chairs for the press. Frank, get onto the GPO and ask them to install extra telephone and fax lines.

Ivy, for the press, I suppose you'd best include them for feeding and watering.'

'Now I will brief the visitors, entertain them and see they are fed and watered, but I still have a pit to run. Because of my broken ankle, I want you, Tommy, to take charge of the underground visit. Oh, and Tommy, tell the men to watch their language. I am sure MPs are probably used to swearing but I don't want them to hear any on this visit. '

'We will, of course, require clean drinking-water for the underground visit. Could you also please arrange that?'

'Leave it to me, Mr Sankey, I'll not let you down. And I'll make sure the men are on their best behaviour,' Tommy added.

With that the Manager dismissed the meeting and everyone returned to their work.

As Bill and Robert returned to their offices, Bill said. 'Robert, who's this PR woman who's coming early?'

'Well, Bill, she's called Elizabeth Hardy and she sounds very nice.'

'Sounds like she's made an big impression on you, Robert. Be careful, you know what those southern girls are like.'

'Well I hope she is as attractive as she sounds on the telephone.'

On returning to his office Robert noticed that there was a fax message in the machine and was delighted to see that it was from Elizabeth, asking him to ring her back.

'Hello, Elizabeth, it's Robert again. You wanted to speak to me?'

'Oh, hello Robert. Well you are meeting the Deputy Chairman in his office at ten o'clock tomorrow morning and I have managed to get you an appointment at No.10 Downing Street with the Prime Minister's Secretary for three o'clock the day after. I hope that's alright, Robert.'

'That's fine, Elizabeth. Well done. Is that it? If so, I will see you tomorrow.'

'Bye, Robert, see you tomorrow.'

# *Eight*

The following day the train from Wigan arrived at Euston station on time and Elizabeth was waiting as promised under the station clock.

She had chosen to wear a beautiful cotton floral dress of ivory with pink and blue flowers, a lovely cut collar and full circular skirt, and as she stood under the clock, many of the passing men glanced back to admire her.

Robert stepped off the train and walked down the platform carrying a leather briefcase.

Elizabeth examined every person coming through the ticket gate, searching for Robert. The only person she could see in the near-distance was a tall, dark-haired handsome man who looked in his late-twenties. Please, God, let that be him, he's absolutely gorgeous she thought.

'Elizabeth?' the man enquired, and as she was still reeling from his good looks, she gave a gentle nod of her head.

'Good. Hello, Elizabeth, I am very pleased to meet you. It was so good of you to come to meet me.'

She gazed into his sparkling blue eyes, and noticed he was wearing a neatly pressed dark suit with a blue striped tie which, coupled with his well-groomed jet-black hair and his strong bearing, gave him an air of comforting sophistication. His aftershave was strong but smelled good.

Quickly recovering her composure she said, 'Oh I am glad to help; we want this visit to be a big success.'

He held out his hand for her to shake, but she ignored it and gave him a kiss on both cheeks instead, having to rise on to her toes to do so.

Robert was pleasantly surprised but tried not to show it.

'Right, I have a staff car outside so let's be on our way.'

'Lead the way, Miss Hardy.'


During the journey they easily chatted about the forthcoming arrangements and were soon at the National Coal Board Head Office in Grosvenor Place.

Hobart House was a big, imposing building, and as the car drew up, at its front a uniformed commissionaire stepped forward and opened the rear door. As Elizabeth stepped out, he smartly saluted. 'Good morning, Miss Hardy.'

'Good morning to you too, Henry,' she said.

As Robert got out of the car she turned to the commissionaire and said, 'This is Mr Robert Kilpatrick, who has an appointment with Sir Alf Kenyon.'

'Good morning, Sir. Welcome to London and Hobart House,' said Henry, before giving Robert a smart salute.

'Good morning, Henry, thank you.'


With Henry taking the lead, Elizabeth and Robert entered the building.

'OK, Robert, I think we have time for a coffee before your appointment. Come to my office.'

They took the large, mahogany lift, which rose slowly to the third floor.

Elizabeth took them through two large doors and through a large office, where several desks were arranged in rows.The staff working at the desks looked on inquisitively as Elizabeth and Robert walked through and went into Elizabeth's Office.

'Milk and sugar, Robert?' she asked, as she walked over to a large coffee machine.

'Milk, no sugar please, Elizabeth.' She reached for two cups, poured them both a coffee to which she added milk.

'Now, sit down Robert, and tell me how long you will be in London.'

Taking a seat opposite Elizabeth's desk, as she took her own seat behind it, he replied, 'Well, just today and tomorrow. There is so much to arrange at the colliery, I must return as soon as I can.'

Sipping her coffee she said, 'Do you want me to book you a hotel room or have you already made a reservation?'

'No, thank you, Elizabeth. My family have an apartment in London, so I will be staying there tonight.' Hesitatingly he continued, 'Look, tomorrow, before seeing the Government representative, would I be presumptuous to ask if I could take you for lunch?'

'Oh, that would be lovely, Robert, I should be delighted.'

'Great, and is the Hilton Hotel alright? They serve a lovely lunch.'

'The Hilton would be fine. What time shall I meet you there?'

'Can you make it for eleven forty-five? I will meet you in the foyer.'

'Eleven forty-five it is, Robert.'

Finishing his coffee, he stood up and said, 'Right, I'd better go and see Sir Alf.'

'I'll take you up to him now. Best of luck.'

The following day Elizabeth strolled into the Hilton, and Robert rushed forward to greet her.

'Elizabeth, you look stunning again, what a beautiful dress.'

'Thank you, Robert, you look pretty good yourself.'

They had a wonderful lunch and discussed what Sir Alf had said, and the future visit.

Outside the hotel an hour later Elizabeth once again gave him a kiss on the cheek, saying, 'That was wonderful, Robert. I look forward to seeing you in Wigan.'

As she left the building she turned, smiled and gave him a wave.

Robert's mind was in a whirl. He smiled back and waved and thought to himself how much he too was looking forward to seeing Elizabeth in Wigan.

Later, after a successful meeting with the Government Secretary at Downing Street, Robert set off to catch his train to Wigan.

Arriving at Euston he was surprised to see Elizabeth waiting on the station concourse.

'Elizabeth, what a surprise. Is anything wrong?'

'No, Robert. I knew you planned to catch this train. What it is, there's been a slight development. The Deputy Chairman has asked me to visit the colliery on the Friday before the visit, and personally finalise the arrangements and set up a press and media office, so I will have to find a local hotel to stay at until the following Wednesday. Can you help?'

'Leave it to me, Elizabeth. I would be happy to help. I know just the place, in fact. The owner is a friend of mine. Do you want me to book a room until the following Wednesday?'

'That would be great, Robert. Thank you, please do that, I will be taking the train on the Friday and will let you know the train time.'

'Excellent, I'll give my friend a ring when I get back.'

'My knight in shining armour,' she joked, 'you don't know how relieved I am, for having you helping me. I have never been to Lancashire and would have been like a lost sheep.'

They parted again and Robert caught his train to Wigan.

# *Nine*

Nurse Annie Belshaw was Redman's full-time nurse and as such was in charge of the Ambulance Room, located near to the pithead baths.

Twenty-eight years old, she had a trim figure, with an ample bust and was considered quite beautiful.

Annie was healthy, with a radiant, tanned face, with intensive blue eyes slanting slightly at the corners, which had a hypnotic effect on anyone seeing her for the first time. She kept herself fit by taking long walks in the surrounding country with her sheepdog, Bess.

She had carried out her nurse's training at Leigh Infirmary, starting as a trainee nurse and rising to the position of Ward Sister. Although she loved her job at the hospital, when offered the job as Redman's Colliery Nurse, she'd jumped at the opportunity.

Her duties at the mine were to provide and maintain the medical services, give first-aid treatment to any injured miners, and to ensure, in the event of any major underground injury, that an ambulance was waiting at the surface when the injured miner was stretchered to the surface to be rushed to hospital.

In addition, Annie was also the First Aid trainer for the miners who were designated First Aiders and had to be re examined every three years.

She ran the courses on behalf of the St John Ambulance Brigade.

Annie had great success in the job, and was a highly valued member of the colliery's management team.

Nearly all the men at the pit professed to be in love with Annie and many had unsuccessfully tried to date her. She has rejected all, but had a secret crush on Roundall, who had regularly attended her first-aid training course in his role as a part-time mines rescuer. However Roundall was completely unaware of this secret. Although he really fancied her, he thought, wrongly, that a woman as beautiful and intelligent as Annie was way out of his league.


It was six-thirty on Wednesday night and Annie had arranged a refresher course for Redman's existing First Aiders, at the nearby Miners Welfare Club.

She had arrived early and was busy setting out the committee room, by positioning large blankets on the floor around the room, and was now positioning piles of triangular bandages at each blanket position.


Tonight she had twenty men attending, including Roundall, Tommy 'Thunder', and Alan Pryce and Horace Brown — two of Roundall's mates. and they had just started to drift in.

Consulting her clipboard list she ticked them off as they arrived. When all twenty were present she stood in front of the group.

'Right, lads, we're going to start with bandaging, so I want you to pair off and when you have found a partner choose a blanket and one of you act as casualty. The casualty should lie down and the other place a triangular bandage around your partner's thigh.'

Later, when she walked around to check their bandaging she was amazed to find that one man had placed the bandage around the casualty's eyes. 'What the blazes have you done, man?' she cried.

'You said to put the bandage round th' eyes, Nurse,' spluttered the man.

'You silly sausage,' laughed Annie 'Wash your ears out. I said put the bandage around his thighs.'

Needless to say the rest of the class was in uproar.

The course finished at nine o'clock and as the men were leaving the room Annie quietly approached Roundall, and asked if he would help her collect the equipment together and carry it to her car.

As Roundall and his two mates had agreed to have a couple of pints in the Club after the course, Roundall said to them, 'See you in a few minutes, lads. I'll just help Annie to tidy up here.'

The men drifted out of the room and Annie and Roundall started to gather the various pieces of equipment together, placing it into her large holdall.

His two mates, Alan and Horace, found a table near the bar. Dick Wayne, though uninvited, pulled out a chair and joined them.

Dick Wayne worked at Redman's and was disliked by most of the men at the pit. With raised eyebrows, Alan looked across at Horace, who just shook his shoulders, so Alan waved over to the bar steward, who a few minutes later brought them over three pints of best bitter on a tray, — the most popular drink in the Club.

Tommy Green stood alone at the bar, with one foot on the

brass floor rail, nursing a pint of Guinness. Although he had taken an active part in the First Aid course with the other three men, as a matter of protocol, Tommy, as Undermanager, never allowed himself to socialise with the workmen.

A few minutes later Annie and Roundall emerged from the committee room, Roundall carrying the heavy holdall.

As they left the Club, Annie cheerfully shouted, 'Good night, lads.'

'Night, Annie' they replied in unison.

'Lads, I'll not be a minute. Get me a pint of bitter in,' Roundall shouted back to the group at the table.

'Are you sure about that? joked his Welsh friend.

'She's a good one, is our Annie,' Alan commented to the group and they all nodded in agreement.

Dick Wayne then came out with, 'See Manager Sankey's broke his ankle. Pity it wasn't his bloody neck!'

The rest of the men suddenly went quiet, as they knew that Tommy, standing at the bar with his back to them, would have overheard the remark.

Turning quickly, in two long strides Tommy strode over to Dick Wayne, grabbed him by his lapels and physically lifted him out of his chair. Tommy's face was bright-red and his eyes blazed with anger. With his nose against Dick's face he shouted, 'Listen, shit brains. Bill Sankey is a good man, he is the best Manager I have ever worked with and is good for Redman's and its men, if only thy had the brains to see that.'

All the men knew of Tommy's boxing past and fiery temper, and Alan Pryce jumped up, putting a restraining arm on Tommy saying, 'Pay him no heed, Tommy, we all know that with him it's gob before brain.'

53

'No, no, no T-T-Tommy,' stammered Dick. 'I agree he's a good bloke. I didn't mean it like that.'

Tommy stared at him for a full thirty seconds, and suddenly let go of Dick's lapels and pushed him back so that he collapsed into his chair, breathing heavily.

Tommy turned and returned to his place at the bar, and calmly continued to sip at his pint of Guinness.

Fred, the Club steward, with a look of concern, looked at Tommy's face, but in return received a grin and a secret wink.

'You daft bugger, Dick. Keep thee gob shut,' said Alan to him. 'Tommy would have ripped thee head off.'

Just then Roundall came in and as he approached the table Alan said,'There's one in pump, Roundall.'

'Cheers, Alan,' Roundall said as he approached the bar where the steward started to pull his pint.

'All reet, Tommy?' he said in greeting to the undermanager.

'Aye, not bad, Roundall lad. Thy seems to be getting on well with that Nurse.'

'Nay,Tommy, just helping her out, she's just a nice person.'

'Well she spent a lot of time showing thee how to tie a proper reef knot. Perhaps that's symbolic, eh?'

'Bollocks! Tommy, she wouldn't look twice at the likes of me.'

'Perhaps then I should have said symbollocks then.'

They both burst out laughing at Tommy's quick-witted humour.

Still laughing, Roundall joined the other three at the table.

'Now what have you three been up to while I've been

helping a damsel in distress?'

'Don't ask. Dick here put his foot in his mouth, as usual, and Tommy had to put him straight.'

'Will thy never learn, Dick. Thee dad christened thee reet name. Someday thy will come a right cropper.'

The pals each took a long drink, relaxing in their comradeship.

Talk soon moved to their common passion for Rugby League Football and their team's next match.

'Are you all going to match on Saturday?'

'Aye, I'd love to see that Billy Boston play again. I saw him play in his first match against Barrow, and boy, is he fast. The rest stand no chance of stopping him when he starts running down the wing.'

'Aye,' Horace agreed, 'where's he from, I've never heard of him before?'

'Well,' Alan proudly said, 'I read that like me he's a Welshman, and played Rugby Union in Wales and then played in the Army, where Wigan spotted him in 1953. He's a great signing and I reckon that he'll be a great asset for a good number of years. It takes a Welshman to play good rugby.'

Dick Wayne, who lived in nearby Leigh, where supporters considered Wigan Rugby as their enemy, piped up 'That's all very well, but Leigh's signed up a record-breaking Olympic sprinter called McDonald Bailey. He scored a try in his first match, a friendly against Wigan, and Leigh won the match.'

'Aye, but I've heard that's the only game he may ever play. He may be fast but he's rubbish at Rugby League. Now our Billy, my fellow Welshman, knows rugby, inside out.'

'Alan,' Roundall retorted, 'Will you stop going on about

being Welsh, it's years since you lived there, and anyway your lot play a different form of Rugby.'

'True,' Alan replied. 'Being Welsh, we do play a different form of the game, but I still don't understand how the game became divided.'

Horace, enthusiastically took his chance to enlighten them. 'Now that's where I can help you. I had a history teacher, at secondary school, who used to play for Warrington and he thought the main event in history was how rugby was split up.'

They all took at sip at their pints and looked at Horace expectantly. 'Go on, Horace, enlighten us.'

'Okay, Alan, I think I can remember it all as he really drummed it into us. We found it much more entertaining than 1066 and all that. What we now call Rugby League started in 1895 as the 'Northern Union' when clubs in the north of England broke away from the Rugby Football Union. The clubs wanted to pay its working class players for time away from work when they played on tours and when they sustained injuries. The sport was considered by the northerners as a toff's sport, especially when the RFU snootily replied that if they cannot afford to play, then they shouldn't play at all. So Rugby League Football was born, the number of players in each team was reduced from fifteen to thirteen players and 'play the ball' was introduced to lessen the need for scrums. The change made Rugby more popular in England, and the increased gate money allowed the clubs to pay benefits to the players and develop their grounds.

Most mining towns had strong teams and a great many miner players became famous. There was a saying locally that when a club was short of forwards, the club coach would go to the top of the pit shaft and shout down, "Send us up two forwards please."

Horace took a deep breath and a long drink of his beer.

Roundall patted him on the back,'Well done, Horace, that was brilliant, thy should go on Mastermind.'

Once all their glasses were empty the pals wandered home.

# Ten

It was Friday night and the Miners Welfare Club was packed. The organist was playing a medley of old popular tunes. Two committee members were sitting at a table near to the stage, nursing their pints.

'This organist is rubbish, just listen to those bum notes,' said Andy, the Club concert secretary.

'Ay,' replied Hugh, 'but he's cheap.' Hugh was the Club's treasurer and now that they were retired, for both men the Club was their lifeblood.

'Do you know, at the last committee meeting the cheeky sod asked for a rise in his fee?'

'Andy, I would recommend that he gets it, that is providing he spends it on music lessons!' laughed Hugh. Andy was just taking a sip of his pint and the comment caused him to spill a bit onto the table, through laughing.

'That's a good 'un, Hugh. Well I only hope this turn I've booked doesn't notice the odd wrong note.'

'Who is she?' asked Hugh.

'Well, she's a local girl. I've heard she's quite good, so I thought I would give her a try, since all that criticism about the quality of the acts I recently booked. I'd better go, she's due on now.'

Andy took a quick sip of his pint and walked to the back of the stage area to talk to Helen King, the local female artist. After a brief word with her Andy walked on the stage, picked up the microphone and switched it on.

'Testing, one two, one two.'

'Before tonight's entertainment can I ask those who have not paid their subs please to do so before the end of the month. We need this money to keep the Club going, so see Hugh with your dues.

Also, this is the last week for you to get names down for the children's Southport trip. This year we've had to book three double-decker Lancashire United Transport buses, so be quick as places are filling up fast.'

'Now, Ladies and Gentlemen, I would like to introduce our turn for tonight. She's a local girl and I know you're in for a treat, but can I ask you to keep the noise down a bit while the turn is on? Now I ask will you please put your hands together for our very own...' He paused and then rather loudly continued, 'Helen King!'

To loud applause as the spotlights came on, Helen walked onto the stage. She was about thirty-five, had a good figure, and was wearing a black figure-hugging cocktail dress that was covered in glittering sequins. The dress was low-cut, partly revealing her ample bust.

Taking the microphone from Andy she fitted it into its stand and turned to the organist with a slight nod. With a large, beaming smile revealing perfect white teeth he started to play her opening number and she belted out Shirley Bassey's 'Big Spender'.

The double doors at the club entrance opened and Roundall

peered in. As he entered he looked around for his fellow workmates. 'Over here, boyo,' shouted Alan Pryce, who immediately received a scowl from the concert secretary.

Roundall made his way around the perimeter of the clubroom to reach his mates' table near the bar. His mates Alan, Big George, Horace Brown, and Ivan the Pole were all seated around the table, which had one empty place.

Alan, remembering the admonishing scowl, whispered across, 'We've saved thee a place,' pointing to the empty chair, 'and I've got you a pint of bitter in as well.'

'Well done, Alan," said Roundall, as he took his place at the table and took a long, slow drink from his glass.

'By Jove, I needed that. Eey, this singer's not bad. She can certainly hit those notes.'

'Big Spender, eh? She can certainly spend a little time with me,' said Horace, eyeing Helen, as he lit a cigarette.

'No chance, Horace. She'd sooner spend time with old Andy over there than with thee,' laughed Big George.

'What about this VIP visit in a couple of weeks? Even our Tory Prime Minister is coming,' continued Horace. 'Cheeky sod! Coming here when he's trying to do the coal industry down.'

'I don't know,' said Roundall. 'Talk among the management and the unions at the rescue training session the other day was that they feel it could be a good opportunity to be able to influence him by pulling out all the stops, making it a big success. I know they will have a go at making him reconsider his policy.'

'Balls, Roundall, he's only doing it for the publicity – one in the eye for the Labour Party, it being their strongest area,' said Alan.

In unison they all picked up their glasses and took a drink, just as the singer started a slow ballad in a deep, husky, sexy voice.

'Oh God, she's driving me crazy,' moaned Horace.

'You're already crazy!' responded Ivan the Pole.

Just then the doors slowly opened and two attractive young ladies came into the Club. Big George looked up and exclaimed, 'Eey up, look who's just walked in, it's Nurse Annie Belshaw and her mate Julie. By gum, Annie's looking fit.'

Horace, with his mouth hanging open, said, 'Aye, and her mate's not bad either.'

'Randy sod, first the singer, and then Annie's mate. Calm down, Horace, before you burst a blood vessel,' said Roundall.

'Okay, but Roundall, I know thy's set thi cap at Annie for a long time. Why don't you do something about it? Like go over and chat her up.'

'No, it's true, I do fancy her, but she would never look twice at a big ugly sod like me, and besides I'm too shy.'

Alan butted in 'Ay, it's true. Thy art a big ugly sod, but how do you know unless you try! Go over with some excuse and then offer to buy them a drink.'

'I don't know. I'll muck it up, said Roundall.

'Go on, you big softy. Get over there,' Alan urged. "What have you got to lose?'

Roundall reluctantly rose from his seat and ambled over towards Annie's table, pretending he was walking past and with a surprised look on his face, said 'Hello, Annie. Nearly didn't see you there. How are you?'

Annie's face lit up at the sight of her big hero and she replied, 'I'm fine, thank you, and this is my mate, Julie.'

'Hello Julie, I'm Roundall. Nice to meet you.'

'And you. I've heard a lot about you from Annie,' she

replied, receiving a sharp kick under the table from Annie in return.

'Oh,' said Roundall, somewhat flustered. "Can I get you ladies a drink?'

'That's very generous of you. Two gin and tonics please," Julie quickly replied.

Roundall headed towards the bar to get the drinks.

'I'll kill you, Julie Marshall,' said Annie, angrily. Now listen here, when he comes back, I want you to go to the toilet and leave us on our own. I have been dying for this chance for ages. And make sure you take your time.'

Roundall returned with their drinks. 'Right, ladies, here you are. I thought you may like ice and lemon in your drink,' He carefully placed the two glasses down on the table.

'Great. Thanks, love,' said Julie, getting up from her chair.

'I'll not be minute. I'm dying for a pee, I'll just go to the toilet.' She walked towards the ladies.

'Sorry about Julie, you can't take her anywhere.'

'That's okay, Annie, she seems alreet. But Annie, there's something I want to ask you,' he said, sitting down in Julie's vacant chair. Annie felt her heart beating faster.

'Yes, Roundall?' she replied, eyes blinking and beaming at him in anticipation.

'Well,' he paused thoughtfully, 'I need a copy of my First Aid Certificate for the rescue service. Can you arrange to get a copy for me please?'

'Certainly,' replied Annie, hiding her disappointment. 'No problem, I'll let you have it.'

Then Roundall blurted out, too quickly and nervously, 'and can I meet you again, just the two of us?'

'Why, Roundall, are you asking me on a date? Because if you are I would like nothing better," she said, noticing the redness in his cheeks.

'Oh great,' he replied, somewhat surprised. 'What shall we do? Pictures?'

'Well I like simple things, like reading, music and taking my sheepdog Bess for long walks at the weekend.'

'We have a lot in common then, Annie. I too like reading and I like nothing better, after a week down pit, than walking in the countryside. How about this Sunday? Say two o'clock, near the old stile, near Lifford Woods.'

'Lovely, Roundall, I'll look forward to it,' she said, grinning as she leaned over and put her hand over Roundall's.


'Ey up, what's this then? You two seem to be getting on well. While the cat's away and all that,' Julie said cheekily as she returned from the toilets.

Roundall reluctantly rose from Julie's chair. 'Well I'd better get back to my mates. I'm really looking forward to meeting Bess on Sunday. See you, girls.' He walked back towards his table near the bar.

Julie looked at Annie, 'From that comment, and the look on your face, you have obviously got a date. Tell me all about it.'


'Hi boyo. How did it go?'

Sitting down, Roundall said, 'I don't believe it, she's actually agreed to go out with me this Sunday!'

'Well done. Told you so. Where are you taking her?' Andy asked.

'We're going for a long walk with her dog, near Lifford

63

Woods.'

'Aye, that's the way to do it. Get her down in the long grass,' Horace said.

Alan looked at Horace with a scowl. 'Now, Horace, she's a respectable young lady. None of that now.' Horace grinned. 'Aye, but she's a nurse and you know what they say about nurses!'


In the centre of the Club sat four old firm friends. There was Billy's mother and father, Edna and Johnny, and their two best friends, Peter and Nellie McKay. Peter worked at the same pit as Johnny and they had all been good friends for many years.

'Did you know Gladys Batty from Coal Pit Lane had died?' Nellie asked them.

'Aye, she was a right character, she'll be missed.'

'Wasn't she supposed to be very clever and something of a poet, but daft as a brush', replied Peter. 'Batty by name, and batty by nature.'

Whereupon, Edna started reminiscing.

'Eey, I'll never forget when I worked on the buses during the war, you know when all the men had gone off to fight and we women replaced them. Well it was so busy that management decided to employ assistant conductresses. I was allocated one and it turned out to be Gladys. I didn't know anything about her then, and I suspect neither did management, especially that she was clever but batty.'

'It was on her first shift, one Monday morning, it would be about 1944, and my bus was on the Croft run. I told Gladys to collect the upstairs whilst I did the downstairs. Save me legs, see.'

'Now when we reached the terminus, I had an arrangement with the landlord at the Black Bull to take all my small change to save me carrying it about, so on leaving the bus, I told Gladys that I would not be long, to stay where she was until I got back. I went into the pub across the road and was away no more than ten minutes.'

'Just as I was leaving the pub I saw to my horror my bus disappearing down the road on its return journey. It would seem that Gladys had got fed up waiting and rung the bus bell three times, which was the signal for the bus to go. My driver, Frank Talbot, thinking it was me ringing it, assumed that all was well and set off. Well, I thought what a carry on. I then ran into the road and in my full conductress uniform and with my ticket machine I flagged down an oncoming motorcycle. Now I must say at this point I was a bit of a looker then.'

'Thy's not so bad now, Edna,' said Peter.

'Thanks for that Peter; pity Johnny here never says that. Anyway, back to the story. I looks at the young bloke on the bike and says, "Quick, my bus's gone off without me, follow that bus." The young man burst out laughing and said, "Get on back, quick." So without any hesitation, I hitched my skirt up, slung my ticket machine around my back and cocked my leg over the saddle and put my arms tight around his waist. "Hang on," he shouted, as he set off after my bus. After a few minutes he caught up with the bus and began to overtake it. When he was level with the driver's cab I began to gesticulating at Frank, who turned and looked at me riding on the back of the motorbike with all my leg showing. He had a stunned expression on his face, and mouthed, "Edna? What's happening" and quickly stopped the bus. I was so relieved that as I got of the bike I gave the motorbike rider a big kiss, full on his lips, and ran to the back of my bus.'

'Needless to say, I gave Gladys the best bollocking she's ever had and when we got back to the depot I told the

Inspector, in no uncertain terms, what he could do with his assistant conductress and that I never wanted to see her face again, God bless her.'

The rest of them were laughing so much they all had tears running down their faces. 'What a story, Edna, it would make a cracking comedy sketch.'

'Every word's true, Nellie, as true as I sit here drinking this bottle of Guinness.'

## *Eleven*

Roundall's mother, wearing a muti-floral pinny and with her hair covered with a red scarf, placed two fried eggs, one sausage, two rashers of dry cured bacon and two slices of Bury black puddings on a warmed white plate as she listened to the omnibus edition of *The Archers*.

Roundall sat at the pine kitchen table only half-listening to the radio, his mind focused on his date with Annie Belshaw later that afternoon.

Turning to the table his mum placed Roundall's regular Sunday fry-up in front of him.

He looked down at his plate, and he saw she had arranged the meal to look like a face — the two eggs as eyes, sausage for the nose, the bacon shaped like a mouth and the round slices of black pudding as small cheeks.

He burst out laughing, remembering his childhood and his mum's great sense of humour.

'Mum,I'm not a kid anymore. I'm twenty-five now.'

'Yer still my little lad even though you're a great big lump now,' she said as she sat down opposite him with her cuppa.

'Thanks, Mum you do a great breakfast. Dad gone fishing then?'

'Yes, he was up at six this morning. Him and his mates have gone off to Flash. I packed him some corned beef sandwiches and a flask last night, so he will be gone a while.

'Roundall, why are you wearing your best sport slacks and that new tee-shirt you bought last week? And do I smell a hint of aftershave? Don't tell me you've got a date at last.'

'Mum, I know you're always on at me to get a steady girlfriend. Well if you must know, yes, I have a date with Annie Belshaw.'

'Oh, wonderful, I know the girl, she the pit nurse at Redman's isn't she? Such a lovely girl and her parents are decent people. And how long has this been going on, you crafty devil?'

'I have been dying to ask her out for ages but have only recently plucked up the courage. Much to my surprise she agreed, so it's early days.'

'Eey, well I never. Perhaps someday I may have grandchildren after all.'

'Mum, calm down, it's our first date remember. We'll see how it goes.'

'Now you be careful, she's a decent girl . Don't be doing or saying anything daft to upset her. Oh ,I'm reet chuffed.'


Annie was early at the stile and she passed the time by throwing a ball which Bess, her faithful sheepdog, chased before grabbing it in her mouth and rushing back to her. Bess dropped the ball at Annie's feet and lay there looking up at her with great big soppy eyes and her head to one side.

'Last time, Bess', she said. As she threw it again she saw Roundall approaching in the distance. She felt her heart flutter as he returned her wave.

As he came closer he saw that she wore a bright-blue summer skirt, which seemed to flare outwards from her waist and finished just above her knees and a matching striped short-sleeved blouse; blue casual shoes completed her outfit.

As she waved again he thought that she looked stunning.

He bent down to greet Bess and stroked her. Bess sat down and looked up at him before raising her right paw for him to shake.

'Oh, that means she likes you; she only does it to people she takes to.'

'Pleased to meet you, Bess.' Bess responded by wagging her tail.'

'Annie, I like the outfit. You look great.'

'Thank you, kind Sir. I've never seen you dressed up; you scrub up quite nice yourself.'

They both laughed easily and climbed the stile and set off to walk towards the woods, Bess following behind.

Roundall was only used to talking, joking and telling stories with men, and usually found it difficult to make smalltalk with women. However with Annie the conversation flowed and seemed so natural as they busily chatted away admiring the beautiful scenery.

'Annie, I read an article in the local newspaper reporting that a white blackbird has been seen in these woods recently.'

'A white blackbird? Get away, you're pulling my leg.'

'As much as I would love to pull your leg, yes, that's what it said. It's been seen several times over the last few weeks.'

They reached an area that had recently been cleared and they sat down on a fallen log and Roundall stroked Bess's head.

The woods had belonged to a local squire who had many years ago donated it to the local community and the local council now maintained it. Besides the natural woods they had constructed two tennis courts, a crown bowling green and a children's' play area, which was well used by the children. The woods were a haven for wildlife.

Roundall suddenly whispered

'Annie, don't move. Look over there,' and he pointed to a large oak tree.

'Where? I can't see anything?'

'There, on the second branch of that large tree, see it?'

'No, I still can't see anything.'

Roundall leaned towards her until the side of his head was touching hers. He put his arm around her and, taking hold of her right hand, pointed her arm towards the great oak tree.

'See the second branch up,' he whispered.

'Oh! My God it's the phantom white blackbird, it's absolutely lovely, how beautiful.'

Turning they looked into each other's eyes. As his deep-blue eyes studied her she could not remember ever experiencing this intensely powerful emotion.

It seemed a simple impulsive action as they slowly brought their lips together in a gentle and loving kiss. It touched Annie so deeply that she let out a gentle moan.

Oh, Annie, lovely Annie,' he whispered softly, brushing a stray hair from her forehead

'What are we doing? I am crazy about you.' Pulling her close he gently kissed her forehead.

'Roundall, love, I have never stopped thinking of you. I never thought you saw me this way.'

'Annie, I have worshipped you from afar for ages, and for

a long time have tried to build up the courage to ask you out but couldn't risk you rejecting me.'

'You silly sausage. I have tried for ages to encourage you. Just look at all the time we have wasted.'

Overcome by a wave of emotion, tiny tears began to trickle down her cheeks. He kissed one of the tears and pulled her nearer to him. She responded instinctively, sinking into his body.

They stayed there for about an hour, neither speaking, just happy and content in each other's embrace.

Holding hands they strolled back through the park entrance and he walked Annie and Bess home.

At the garden gate they arranged to see each other in a few days.

Annie waved to Roundall as he walked away and turned to walk to her front door. Wow! she thought, walking on air. This must be love she told herself.

Although they both hoped that their paths might cross later in the week at Redman's Colliery, little did they know that that would be in circumstances that neither of would have ever dreamed of.

# *Twelve*

It was the following Friday, 13th May, and Robert Kilpatrick was anxiously pacing up and down the platform at Wigan station in anticipation of the arrival of Elizabeth Hardy. The tannoy announced the arrival of the two-twenty train from London Euston. He walked slowly along the platform and in the distance saw the train approaching. It slowed to a crawl before coming to a screeching halt alongside him. The stationmaster shouted, in a broad Lancashire accent, 'Wigan Station.' The doors opened and Robert scanned the people descending onto the platform, looking for the young lady he had come to meet.

He was really excited about seeing her again and began to worry that she may have missed the train when, at the far end of the platform, through the steam, emerged a beautiful vision. Elizabeth was wearing a bright primrose-yellow summer dress and carried a small leather case. With her trim figure and yellow outfit he thought she looked like a beautiful ray of sunshine.

Elizabeth had spent a considerable amount of time trying to decide what to wear for her trip to Lancashire. For the press conference she had selected a smart dark suit with a tailored jacket and a straight skirt. She had also packed two summer dresses and for the journey had chosen her favourite primrose-yellow summer dress with matching belt. The dress was short, although not too short, and showed off her legs. She had a twinkle in her eye in anticipation of meeting Robert Kilpatrick.

She had enjoyed the journey up as the Coal Board had allowed her to travel First Class. In the restaurant car, she had enjoyed a starter of smoked salmon with a niçoise salad, a rack of lamb with steamed vegetables for the main, and to finish with, strawberries smothered in cream. She had allowed herself a half-bottle of red wine, although she would be paying for the wine herself.

It was a bright sunny day and as she watched the countryside fly past, she found herself reflecting, and appreciating how she came to be in this position.

As she was trying to complete The Times crossword, the conductor came along to announce that they were now approaching Wigan station. She was excited and couldn't wait to see Robert again.

'Elizabeth?' Robert shouted, and as he was still reeling from her good looks, she gave a wave and ran towards him.

'Oh, Robert, it's wonderful to see you again. I have been so looking forward to it.'

She gazed into his sparkling blue eyes and noticed he was wearing a dark-blue blazer, blue shirt and light sports trousers. She recognised his aftershave from the last time they'd met.

'It's so good of you to come and meet me.'

'May I take your case, Madam,' he joked with formality. 'Your carriage awaits.' She easily slipped her arm into his and they strolled down the platform towards the exit.

'I have booked a room for you at the Manor House until Wednesday, so I will take you there now in my car. When

73

you have inspected your room, how about a coffee and a chat?'

Smiling brightly she replied, 'Excellent, Robert, Let's go.'

They left the station entrance and Robert guided her to the car park and towards a shiny bright-red Morgan sports car.

'Is that your car, Robert?' she almost squealed.

'Yes it is. It's a Morgan Plus 4, and it was a present from my grandfather on my becoming a Chartered Accountant.'

'It's fantastic. I like the bright-red colour. Your grandfather must think a lot of you, besides being incredibly wealthy.'

After putting her case in the boot Robert held the passenger door open for her and as Elizabeth climbed in he couldn't help but notice her shapely legs. When he was settled in the driver's seat, still reflecting on her legs, he said, 'Yes, I will tell you all about my family over coffee, and I would like to know more about you. I love this car but wait until you feel the wind in your hair.'


Robert drove the Morgan with an assured confidence and Elizabeth smiled as she listened to the throaty roar of the exhaust as they drove to the outskirts of Wigan. They eventually arrived at a pair of huge wrought-iron gates and Robert drove through the gates on to a wide, gravel drive. In the distance they could see a magnificent building.

'Wow! Robert, is that where I'm staying? It looks like a country manor house.'

'Yes, Elizabeth, it was and it's now called The Manor House. And you are correct, it was originally built as a manor house for the local Earl who owned all the coal mines in the Lancashire area, however when the mines were nationalised the Earl sold up and moved his entire estate to Cheltenham.'

Crunching on the gravel, Robert parked the car at the front of the hotel. He helped Elizabeth out and retrieved her case from the boot. They walked up the flight of stone steps leading to the entrance door, Elizabeth again linking Robert in a confident and completely natural manner.

Once in the foyer they both stopped in their tracks and gazed up to look at an enormous crystal chandelier, which glittered in the natural light.

'Beautiful,' gasped Elizabeth.

'Robert,' a voice shouted from across the foyer and turning they saw a smartly-dressed man with greying hair walking quickly towards them with his right hand outstretched.

'Robert, my friend, it is good to see you and is this the visitor from the big city you were telling me about?' Smiling, he shook Robert's hand, and warmly continued, 'But you didn't tell me how attractive she was.'

Elizabeth smiled and looked at Robert's blushing face.

'Come on, Lambert, stop trying to embarrass me. Let me introduce Miss Elizabeth Hardy, Head of the National Coal Board's Public Relations department. Elizabeth, this is Lambert Dean, owner of six major hotels and dear friend of mine.'

Greeting Elizabeth, Lambert gave a slight bow, kissed the back of her hand and said, 'Miss Hardy, I am delighted to meet you. Welcome to the Manor House.'

'Elizabeth, please, Mr Dean, and I love your building.'

'Lambert, please. Yes it really is a magnificent building. I have allocated you the best room in the hotel and it is now ready for you. Would you like to check-in or would you like to view the room first?'

'Looking at the immaculate condition of your hotel I'm

sure I don't need to inspect it, I'm sure it will be excellent, Lambert. However Robert and I will be taking coffee to discuss the proposed VIP visit to the colliery."

'Excellent. I will sign you in. Robert will show you the way to the lounge and I will arrange for coffee to be brought to you.'

Robert led Elizabeth to the lounge and as they entered Elizabeth stopped, and gazed around the room. The lounge walls had oak half-panelling, above which was rich floral wallpaper. Around the room were large pictures of local scenes, mainly of the Wigan and Leigh area, and many showing mining scenes from the past. A large, coal fire burned in an ornate fireplace above which was hung a sizable portrait of a portly gentleman, who she presumed was the Earl, the original owner. Scattered in groups around the room were brown and green Queen Ann-style leather chairs and, along two sides, enormous Chesterfield sofas.

'Robert, it's like a London Gentleman's Club.'

'Yes, Elizabeth, I sometimes think that, when I call for coffee on a Saturday morning for a chat with Lambert,' replied Robert, as he guided her towards two leather chairs in the corner. As they sat down a girl in a black dress and white apron approached, carrying a tray. Smiling, she said, 'Your coffee, Mr Kilpatrick. I've brought you hot milk as usual and also cream, in case the lady would prefer that.'

'Thank you, Millie, as efficient as ever.' The girl smiled at Robert and placed the tray on the table in front of them and quietly left the lounge.

'Well, Robert, you seem to be at home here and that girl certainly has a crush on you.' Much to Robert's surprise she continued, 'It seems that I may have some competition.'

Robert coughed and quickly grabbed the coffee pot, not knowing how to respond to Elizabeth's remarks.

'Shall I pour, Elizabeth? Milk or cream?'

'Oh, milk please, Robert. I also prefer hot milk in my coffee, but no sugar please. Now please tell me your life story.'

Robert carefully poured the coffee, added the hot milk, and placed the cup and saucer in front of Elizabeth. Picking up his own cup he sank back into the leather chair.

'Before I start, Elizabeth, have a sip of your coffee and then I'll tell you some of my family history.'

Elizabeth smelled the coffee, took a small sip, and then slowly swallowed it. Her eyes suddenly opened wide and she gasped, 'Wow! What is this coffee? I've never tasted coffee so good.'

'Ah,' said Robert. 'That's where the story starts — with coffee. In the early eighteen hundreds my great-grandfather started a tea-importing business in London. With tea being very popular and expensive at that time, the business was a great success. He went on a trip to Jamaica to see an old school friend who had recently been appointed as the Governor there, and that is where he first tasted this coffee. Like you, the coffee impressed him because of its exceptional sweetness, its aroma, rich flavour, full body, and mild acidity, so he arranged for a shipment to be sent to his company in London. The coffee took London by storm, so he arranged regular shipments.'

'The coffee is called Blue Mountain coffee, because it thrives in the rich, fertile, volcanic soil and the island's misty cover shades it from the burning sun.'

'Great-grandfather made a fortune, and due to his contact in Jamaica, he became the UK's sole distributor of this fine coffee. In about 1860 he sold the business for around two million pounds. Today, Blue Mountain coffee is considered the best coffee in the world, and is even served in the White House. And of course Lambert only serves the best. Sorry about the history lecture, Elizabeth.'

'No, Robert, it's a fascinating story, and I agree it's the best-tasting coffee I have ever had. But what happened next?'

'Well, Great-grandfather decided to retire and hand over to his son, my grandfather of course, who could see that banking was rapidly expanding and was probably where the future was developing. So he invested all the money in starting a bank in the family name. His Midas touch worked once again and the bank became one of the largest in the financial world.

My family are still in banking, but today mainly operating in the merchant banking sector.'

'I went to private school, in fact the same school as my father and grandfather attended, something of a family tradition. I did rather well at school and although my father wanted me to join the family business, I had set my heart on becoming a doctor and was all signed-up to start my studies at Edinburgh University Medical School.'

However, in 1941, along with thousands of other young men, I received in the post my call-up papers to serve King and Country. On opening them, it was a shock to find I had been called up to the coal mines. As you are probably aware working for the coal Board, this was a government move, introduced by the then Minister of Power, Ernest Bevin, to ensure that the mines kept producing much-needed coal for the war effort.

My family, with all their contacts, tried to get the placement changed, but to avail; I became a Bevin Boy.'


'Somewhat surprisingly, I loved it. I spent my first six months underground and must say that the great camaraderie was something I hadn't experienced before. I took to mining like a duck to water. I loved its people and the bond that developed between the hard-working miners.

My family are somewhat disappointed that I have still not joined the banking business and they live in hope, but for the present I am content with my life.'

'Robert, you would have made a great doctor and I am certain your surgery waiting room would have been full, of women patients at least,' she teased.

'Right lady, enough of me. What about you. Are there any men in your life?'

Elizabeth blinked her eyes.

'No, Robert, there are no men in my life at the moment, so there could be a vacancy,' she said, looking into his blue eyes and laughing as he blushed once again.

'Daddy was a leading barrister in London and is now a High Court Judge; Mummy is a very strong, determined woman and is the head teacher of an independent girls' school in Essex. I had a good education and went on to gain a First Class Honours degree at Oxford University. Soon I was fortunate to be offered a position at Hobart House and as you know I am now the head of the NCB's Public Relations department. I love my job and have a great team working for me. I have a small flat in Kensington and I like to play chess, drink good wine, visit theatres, read and complete crosswords, okay?'

'Lovely, Elizabeth. I too play chess. I will challenge you to a game sometime.'

They sat relaxing and sipping their coffee for a while, until Robert said, 'I think it's time that I checked on what's happening at Redman's Colliery. I'll ask the hotel manager to show you to your room and take your case up. Now we have the whole weekend in front of us, we can leave the VIP visit details until Monday. I know a nice little French restaurant not far away. What time would you like me to pick you up? Say seven, to dine at eight o'clock, would that be okay? And I'll use father's Bentley, then you will be more comfortable.'

'I cannot wait, Robert. And thank you for meeting me and taking good care of me.'


At precisely seven o'clock Robert drove the Bentley into the drive of the Manor House Hotel. Elizabeth came out and Robert got out of the car and opened the passenger door for her. 'Gosh, this is real luxury,' she said as she sank into the soft leather passenger seat.

They enjoyed a cosy meal in the French restaurant and at about eleven o'clock Robert drove back to the front door of the hotel.

'Robert, that was a wonderful evening. Are you coming in for a drink? Oh, but you are driving. Sorry!'

'Ah, now, Elizabeth, I have arranged with Lambert to have a room for tonight, so I can really relax and now I intend to have a large brandy and a fine cigar.'

'Mr Kilpatrick, you haven't booked a room with an adjoining door have you?' she mocked.

'No, I have not, Miss, but my room is on the same floor as yours.'

They walked arm in arm into the hotel and in the lounge found their favourite corner chairs.

Robin, the night duty waiter approached. 'Good evening, Mr Kilpatrick. Would you like to order any drinks?'

'Yes please, Robin. I will have a large glass of your finest brandy and would you please bring the cigar selection box please. Elizabeth?'

'Yes, I too will have a large brandy, but I will pass on the cigar thank you.'

They both settled back into their deep comfortable leather chairs and Elizabeth said, 'What a fantastic meal that was. I am amazed that such quality of food exists outside London.'

'Yes, it is exquisite. The chef, André Gerard, had a very successful two-Michelin-star restaurant in Paris but, because his father was Jewish, when the Germans were on the outskirts of Paris during the war, he decided to flee Paris for Britain and all his dedicated staff came with him. He found his present restaurant, which was a ruined country house, and with the money his family managed to escape with, he bought it. He and his staff took two years to renovate the building and, much to the amazement of the locals, he opened a French restaurant here in Lancashire. Even with rationing, his dishes became very popular. The rest is history and over the years his fame and reputation has become legendary. He even has French people coming over just to dine with him. He loves the area and its people, and as you probably noticed, speaks English with a unique French and Lancashire accent.'

'What a wonderful story. Here come our drinks, Robert.'

With a flourish, Robin placed the glasses of brandy on the table and presented the box of cigars to Robert. Opening the box, Robert selected a King Edward, picked up the cutter, and snipped the tip off the narrow end of the cigar. Robin produced a box of matches, struck one and Robert leaned forward to light his cigar.

'Ahh, thank you, Robin. As efficient as ever.'

'My pleasure, Mr Kilpatrick,' replied Robin, as he closed the box and walked away.

They picked up their brandy balloon glasses and clinked them together. 'Cheers, darling,' said Robert, and they both took a sip.

Cupping his brandy in his hand Robert remarked, 'You know, I love the feel and shape of a brandy glass, and as you cup the glass your hand has a gently warming effect on the liquid.'

'You know what Daddy always says about that? He says that men feeling the shape of the glass in their cupped hand reminds them of caressing a woman's breast.' She burst out laughing when she saw the shocked look on Robert's face.

They spent a pleasant hour chatting about their likes and dislikes as they sipped their drinks.

Eventually they decided it was time to retire and they slowly ascended the oak stairs to their floor.

They arrived at Elizabeth's room and she leaned against the doorframe and looked into Roberts blue eyes. Like two attracting magnets their lips were slowly drawn to each other. The kiss was soft and gentle with their lips slightly parted. Elizabeth sighed and suddenly they were both filled with a great rapture, the kiss becoming full and passionate.

Robert could feel his ardour building up and tried in vain not to let Elizabeth feel the increasing swelling in his lower region.

Parting for breath Elizabeth laughingly whispered, 'Oh, Robert those oysters you had are certainly working.'

She quickly slid her key in the lock and opened her bedroom door. Grasping his hand she led him into her room. She closed the door and switched on the lights and they started kissing passionately again. Slowly pushing him away and looking into his eyes she murmured, 'Robert, I think I'm falling in love with you."

"Oh, Elizabeth, I feel exactly the same way, I haven't stopped thinking of you since we met in London, but I think I should now return to my room."

"Come on, Darling, we are both mature adults who are

madly in love. She opened her wardrobe and she took out a white towelling dressing-gown saying, 'Change into this and relax while I change into something sexy,' and then walked to the bathroom.

Robert quickly undressed and slipped on the dressing-gown and stretched out onto the large bed.

After a few minutes Elizabeth stood in the doorway of the bathroom looking and smiling at Robert. As he looked up, he saw her in a fine full-length silk negligée, the light from the bathroom behind her shining through the gown, revealing her perfectly-shaped body with a slender waist.

Robert swallowed and felt slightly giddy as he looked on in rapture before exclaiming, 'My goodness, you look ravishing, Miss Hardy.'

Giggling like a schoolgirl, she ran to the bed and jumped on to it and turned to lie alongside him. Robert put his left arm around her shoulder and gently kissed her on the lips as he placed his right hand on one of her breasts. He felt the breast swell up and the nipple harden under his touch. Still kissing her he moved his hand slowly down her body coming to rest on the mound between her legs. He then gently moved his fingers backwards and forwards, until she suddenly broke the kiss and gasped, 'Go easy, Robert! or it will all be over too soon.'

Pushing his hand away she snatched his robe open and grasped at his proud erection.

'My goodness, Robert, that could hold up the roof on a coal face.'

They both laughed and Elizabeth then pulled up her nightdress and climbed astride him and carefully guided him into her.

Robert lay there with his eyes closed as she started to slowly rise up and down, driving him further into her. He opened his eyes to watch, then reached forward and began to massage her shapely breasts. As she moved faster and faster he groaned with pleasure. He desperately tried to hold back his passion, wanting it to last forever but mainly not to reach a climax too soon. Suddenly he realised that she was on the point of fulfilment and he let his restraint go. He felt an explosive discharge as he came at the same time as Elizabeth and she gave a cry of delight as she too climaxed. Exhausted, she fell gasping at his side and she kissed him lovingly on the cheek.

After a restful period while they were both locked in each other's arms, Robert looking at her smiling and brushed a stray hair from her face.

'Elizabeth Hardy, that was something else, out of this world, and I never want to leave you ever again.'

'Yes, Robert it was wonderful, but sadly my darling, after the visit is over I will have to return to London and we will see little of each other.'

'Now that's where you're wrong, young lady. I have good news. The family banking business is mainly based in London and we have a large family home in Chelsea; we also have an apartment in Mayfair which I can use when I am in the capital. What I plan to do is every Friday, for the foreseeable future, is to catch the intercity train from Wigan to London; it only takes two hours twenty minutes, and stay every weekend at my apartment.'

She jumped up on her knees.

'Robert, that's great, yippee!'

They made love at a more leisurely pace and he returned to his room at about five o clock in the morning.

At the breakfast table next morning, whilst they were enjoying a full English breakfast, Lambert approached, enquiring, 'Good morning, my dears, I hope you both had a good night's sleep.'

'Excellent, thank you, Lambert,' replied Robert.

Elizabeth looked at Lambert and with a twinkle in her eye replied, 'Yes, I too had an excellent night's...' and paused for a few seconds before continuing, 'sleep.'

Lambert left the room grinning and shaking his head.

# *Thirteen*

It was 1920 and Tommy was eleven years old, and with his three best pals, Johnny Jones, Peter McKay and Robin Brown had just started at the local secondary modern school. It turned out to be a great disappointed to them.

At the small junior Methodist school they had attended, everyone knew each other, but at this big school they were like lost souls; it felt like there were not hundreds of kids, but at least a thousand. The teaching was completely different. After being used to having the same teacher for a year, here they had so many different ones, teaching so many different subjects, that they were dizzy with it all.

At regular intervals a loud bell would ring and off they would have to march, in single file, following a narrow path of paving slabs around what the school called cloisters, and woe betide anyone who got out of line, as on each corner of the cloisters, stood a glowering fourth year prefect.

Back home, after tea, the three pals would get together and play outside with other children. Games such as kick-out-can, tick-your-out and piggy were always popular, and sometimes, if they were feeling a bit naughty, knock-and-run.

As darkness approached, shouts could be heard of mothers calling their kids: 'Jimmy, come in, it's bedtime', 'Jack! I'll not tell you again!', 'For God's sake, Sheila!, this is your final warning.'

Everyone had just gone in and Tommy and his three mates were left on their own.

'We must find something better to do; this is boring,' grumbled Tommy.

Enthusiastically, Robin said, 'A lad in my class has just started the Boys Brigade at the Methodist school and he says it's brilliant.'

'What do they do?'

'Well, for a start, they have two football teams — a junior team and a senior team, — then they do first-aid training and boxing. They go to camp at Towyn once a year, with no parents and, wait for it, they have a band of bugles and drums.'

'Sounds great, when do they meet?'

'Tuesday night and Thursday night, my classmate says.'

'Right, let's give it a go next Tuesday.'

The following Tuesday at six forty-five, Tommy, Johnny, Peter and Robin arrived at the schoolroom.

They nervously went in and saw a large number of boys aged between eleven and eighteen smartly marching in formation up and down the schoolroom. Each boy wore a cap, positioned at an angle on the side of his head, a white sash, worn diagonally over his jacket, and a brown leather belt with the Boys Brigade crest on its buckle.

At the front of the hall stood a young officer aged about twenty. He stood to attention, holding a cane under his right arm. When the marching boys reached the top of the hall, he shouted some indistinguishable command and, in unison, the boys performed a manoeuvre which resulted in them marching the opposite way down the hall. The three lads were really impressed.

A voice from the side said, 'Hello, lads, have you come to join us?'

'Yes but we don't know what we do,'said Tommy, acting as spokesman.

'OK, I am the Captain of the company and my name is Mr Franks. First thing, to join you have to be at least eleven years of age.'

'That's OK then, we are all eleven,' Tommy answered.

'Right then, I will sign you up and give you a recruitment card. Now you must attend punctually for eleven weeks. Each week I will teach you the rules of the Boys Brigade, how to do basic drill and how to wear a uniform. Now each of you take one of these Boys Brigade Handbooks, take it home and study it, as it will become your bible for the next eleven weeks. At the end of this time, you will have a test. You'll have to know who the founder of the Boys Brigade was, when he founded it and where and, most important of all, you will have to recite the 'Object of the Boys Brigade' off by heart. Don't look so worried; it's all in the handbook. If you pass this test you will be awarded your first badge — a buttonhole badge, — to wear in your lapel. You will also be allowed to wear a private's uniform. We provide the leather belt, but you must buy the cap and haversack.'

The Captain could see that the three lads were keen to join. 'Right that's enough for now. I suggest you sit at the side of the hall and watch the boys and their activities.'

The lads couldn't believe what they saw in the next two hours: there were first-aid classes, PE, including boxing practice, and the session finished with band practice. The band marched up and down the hall, playing their instruments and Peter remarked later that he felt the hairs on the back of his head stand up when he heard the solo silver bugler playing.

After dismissal, they left the hall and chatted happily as they walked to the bus stop.

'I really enjoyed that,' said Peter. 'I want to learn the bugle.'

'I'm for the drums,' Tommy replied.

'Me too,' said Robin.

'I'm with Peter, bugle for me,' added Johnny.

The bus then arrived, and they jumped on and were soon home. They had much to think about, and felt sure that now they would never be bored again.

That night, Peter dreamed he was playing the silver solo bugle.


Over the next five years the lads grew and blossomed within the Boys Brigade, rising through the ranks.

Tommy become quite a good boxer, winning a couple of boxing medals at the battalion games. Peter even achieved his much-loved silver solo bugle performance.

However, at fifteen, things changed dramatically. It was their final year at secondary school and thoughts turned to work.

The careers adviser from the local authority arrived in school. 'Do you all know what you are going to do when you leave school?,' he asked.

'Sir,' from a girl on the front row, 'I'm going to serve in my dad's sweet shop.'

'Lucky sod,' muttered a boy at the back, 'all them free toffees!'

A red-headed boy at the back piped up, 'I want to be an

electrician, Sir,' and another girl said she wanted to be a secretary.

'Right,' said the careers adviser, 'the young lady working at her dad's shop, now that's good, keeping it in the family. As for those wanting to be electricians, I'm afraid it's bad news. You see, there are ten vacancies for electrical apprentices, same for fitters, and already I know they have had two hundred applicants. So, sorry, lads, the employers will only consider those who went to the Grammar school. As for the secretary, better news there, you will be able to sign on at the Technical College and learn shorthand and typing.'

The careers adviser was in full flow. 'The good news is that the National Coal Board are looking for young men for underground work, and they need a lot. As for the girls, there are still plenty of vacancies in the cotton factories. I have here a number of forms, so if you're interested take one, take it home and discuss it with your parents. Then if you want to take up the offer, fill it in and return it to your teacher tomorrow.'

So it was that the four mates decided to apply for the mines and were told to report for a medical examination the following Monday.

The medical was scheduled for nine o'clock at the local colliery medical room and the four lads turned up on time at the colliery gates.

After asking the way they eventually found the medical room. On opening the door what they saw was complete chaos. There were boys everywhere, all talking at the same time, some taking their shirts off, and other seemingly walking aimlessly around the room.

A nurse, in uniform, and the male Ambulance Room attendant looked harassed and confused.

'Quiet! Everyone, shut up,' the nurse — a large, overweight woman called Sister Silver, shouted at the top of her voice. 'I can't hear myself think.'

The room suddenly went quiet.

'OK,' said the Attendant, 'form a line here.' And when the line had formed, he gave the first five lads a plastic jug. Now you five, go into those cubicles and pee in your jug then take it to Sister Silver over there, near the sink.'

The boys looked at him in amazement, but went to their various cubicles, the other lads chuckling and nudging one another. After a few seconds they came out clutching their jugs steaming with fresh pee. Except for one lad, who moaned, 'Sir, I can't pee.'

'Right, you lot go over there to the Sister, you give me your jug, lad.'

He then handed it to the next lad in the queue, pointing him to the cubicle which was now empty. Speaking to the boy who could not pee, he said, Handing him a pint glass full of water, he said, 'Sit here, lad, and drink all of this and tell me when you feel you want to pee.'

As the lads reported to the Sister, she took their jugs, emptied a little into a cylindrical tube and placed an oblong piece of test paper into the sample. On removing it she compared it to a chart on her table and then wrote down the result.

Without looking up she shouted, 'Next,' as she emptied the jug and gave it a rinse under the tap.

If she had looked up, she would have seen a scene of sheer bedlam. Most of the lads knew each other and were competing for who could be the biggest joker. Some, coming out of the cubicles, were sharing their sample with those going in; those who could nor read the lower letters on the eye chart were quickly dashing up to it, creeping back and putting a hand over one eye and reciting loudly the letters they had memorised.

Tommy and his mates were eventually handed a slip of paper printed with their name, National Insurance Number and date of birth, on which Sister Silver had stamped in the box at the bottom, 'A1 Fit for Underground Work.'

'Right, lads, we are now pitmen. Let's go home,' said Tommy.

Two weeks later they started their ten-week training in an old school building.

After Tommy had completed his training he worked as a haulage lad, where his duty was to connect thirty full tubs of coal to the haulage rope by a chain. This operation was called 'lashing on' and the moving rope then pulled the coupled tubs to the pit bottom, to then be wound up the pit shaft.

Needless to say Tommy soon became bored with this and when he saw a poster advertising further mining training at the local technical college he became interested, especially as it was to be 'day release', and so a chance for a day off from the pit.

He knocked on the door of the colliery Training Officer to get more information.

'Come in,' shouted the Training officer.

The Training Officer was a large, rotund man with thinning hair and a ruddy complexion. He looked at young Tommy and, with a smile on his face, said, 'Yes, lad, who are you and what can I do for you?'

'My name's Tommy Green and I saw a poster advertising College and I would like to go to college, on day release, to study mining, Sir.'

'Right, Tommy, you have come at the right time. Signing

on is this Thursday. Go to the college on Thursday night and sign on for the General Mining course. You'll need to attend three nights a week.'

'But I want day release. I'm not doing three nights a week after working down pit all day.'

'Listen to a wise old man, lad. Sign on for three nights. I know as a fact that they will not have enough students for day release so they will look at anyone keen enough to do three nights a week and offer them day release to make the class numbers up.'

'I don't know, are you sure?,' said Tommy hesitantly.

'Trust me, lad,' replied the Training Officer with a confident smile as he led Tommy out, patting him on the back. 'Trust me.'

So on Thursday night, along with twelve others, Tommy reluctantly enrolled on the night course.

The Training Officer had been correct though, in that the college had only had ten students registered for day release, so the NCB approved that the night students be transferred.

All the twelve that had signed on with Tommy were now on the day release course and Tommy was thrilled to bits.

He was notified that his first class would be the following Thursday, and all week he looked forward to his first day studying.


At eight fifty-five the class of twenty-two new students filed into the classroom at the college.

The teacher stood in front of the class and addressed them with,'Right, boys, find yourself a seat and settle down. Your first lesson is maths.'

He walked to the blackboard and started to chalk on it a

simple algebraic problem, 2b+c= '

'Right, we will start with a simple one. Write the answer in your book.' As the teacher started to write another question, Tommy looked at the blackboard, puzzled. He turned to the lad on his left and started to say, 'That's daft, that's not maths. You can't add letters together.' Hesitating, he looked to the boy who had his head down writing the answer to the set problem.

'Oh, my God, I'm out of my depth here,' he thought. 'What shall I do? There's only one thing for it,' and he raised his right arm.

The teacher looked up,

'Yes, what's the problem, lad?'

'Sir, I've heard the word algebra, but never knew what it meant. I didn't know you could add letters together.'

The teacher hesitated and putting his hand on his forehead said, 'Right, is there anyone else in the same position?'

Nervously, seventeen of the twenty-two students slowly raised their hands.

The teacher paused looking over the class, then took his coat off and hung it on the back of his chair. Walking to the front of the class he put his hands on his hips, 'OK, I see I'm going have to do some teaching. Sorry to those who went to the Grammar school. Right, all pay attention.'

He then cleaned the blackboard and started with the basics of algebra.

The lads, unlike at school, had come to the college to learn, and also as they were being paid for it, they soaked up the lessons and the techniques like a sponge and soon became very proficient at all branches of mathematics, much to the surprise and delight of the teacher, who felt an enlightened feeling towards his teaching, one that he had not felt in a long time.

Tommy progressed through the various courses in the first two years, gaining first prize for the college's 'Mining prize'.

At twenty-two years of age he had taken his exams and practical tests to allow him to be a shotfirer, handling and using explosives down the mine.

The shotfirer's job, as the name suggests, was to charge the holes, that had been predrilled into the coal, inserting explosive charges, and from a safe distance, set off the charges.

This position was the first step to becoming an official of the mine management structure. The next step up was that of 'Deputy', the title of the person in charge of a coalface and its roadways, or district as it was termed. Following Deputy came Overman, the person in charge underground, of the entire district's Deputies. Beyond Overman came Undermanager, who was in charge of all operations underground, being responsible only to the Colliery Manager.


This was Tommy's first week acting as a fully qualified shotfirer and he was determined to make a success of it.

It was common practice in British coal mines for the shotfirer to have a young miner assist him. The young man's role was, at the start of the shift, to carry the heavy, round rubber pouches of explosives powder from the surface explosive magazine to the coalface.

These explosives were tubes, or packets, of gunpowder shaped like a sausage. The contents were tightly packed and wrapped in a strong, waxed paper tube. The explosives were perfectly safe and could be handled roughly without any danger, as they would not explode until a detonator was inserted and detonated by an electrical charge from a battery generator. The young man was commonly called by all a 'powder monkey', a term originating in old Navy days for persons handling gunpowder for the ship's cannon.

The detonators, however, were very dangerous, and had to be treated with extreme care, as even without the powder, if detonated could cause major injury or death.

Therefore the mining regulations required that only the Shotfirer handle the detonators, which he collected personally from the surface powder magazine.

One hundred detonators were neatly placed in individual compartments in an oblong leather case, about nine inches long, which the Shotfirer wore fastened to his belt at all times. He also had a special key to unlock the case.

This being Tommy's first day he and the powder monkey arrived at the coalface where the holes had been drilled for the charges by the previous shift. The two of them climbed on to the low coalface and, on their knees, scrambled to the first of fifty holes.

Assisted by the powder monkey, Tommy rammed and sealed each hole with an explosive charge and connected each detonator's electric leads together into a series connection.

After the last hole had been charged, Tommy connected the leads to a long cable and they then scrambled off the coalface, and ran out the main twin cable for about a hundred yards. For safe refuge they entered a manhole dug into the side of the roadway.

Previously, Tommy had cleared the coalface of all men, who had now retired a safe distance along the return roadway. One of the men had been selected to be a sentry and he clipped a red plastic disc over his cap-lamp. This disc was printed with 'Sentry' in black lettering and the light from the cap-lamp made the red disc glow and would warn any men approaching that shotfiring was about to take place. Another sentry was on duty at the other end of the coalface.

Tommy picked up a small battery generator, which he then connected to the two leads; from his waistcoat pocket he removed his special key and inserted it into the battery.

Quickly looking out of the manhole in both directions, he shouted, 'Firing,' and sharply turned the key.

Normally, at this stage, a massive explosion shook the whole area, followed by dust and smoke. However on this occasion all that he heard was the sound 'fiztt.'

With a creased brow he reinserted the key and turned it again. Still no explosion.

'Shit, a bloody misfire, on my first day,' he cried out.

A shotfiring misfire is a very serious mishap. If it's not simply poor wiring then it could be a faulty detonator, which must then be isolated and recovered. The biggest fear was that if the coal was excavated and the detonator not found, it could be passed on unawares in the coal and sold to a householder and subsequently cause death or major injury.

In desperation Tommy tried another generator, but got the same result.

Leaving the manhole he turned to the powder monkey, 'You stay here, I'm going back to check the wiring.' He followed the cable back to the coalface, examining it in detail for any breaks. He climbed onto the coalface and proceeded to inspect every detonator wiring joint.

Half an hour later he returned to the manhole, covered in sweat, and gasped, 'I don't know what's wrong; I've checked every joint on every charge and they are all okay.'

The powder monkey looked at him and with a puzzled expression said, 'Well it's still not working, I've been trying it whilst you've been away!'

Needless to say, the powder monkey was soon transferred to other duties.

# *Fourteen*

The colliery was a scene of great activity on the Tuesday morning of the VIP visit.

The rescue room bore a new sign saying 'Media Centre' and a group of national and local pressmen were gathered around Elizabeth Hardy. She was handing them a schedule of the visit, along with a press release issued by the National Coal Board press officer.

Alongside the media centre, several large vans were parked in a line, one bearing the legend 'BBC Outside Broadcasting', from which technicians were dragging large cables into the media centre. Scattered around, GPO engineers were climbing telegraph poles and slinging new telephone wires towards the media centre.

Elsewhere the surface foreman was patrolling the area, and issuing last-minute instructions to the various groups of his workmen who were rearranging supplies, gardening, and generally ensuring that the pit looked clean and presentable for the day.

The foreman came across a young apprentice who he had allocated the job of pasting new, brightly-coloured safety posters onto the large notice board located at the bottom of the pit headgear steps.

'No, No! You silly sod! Put it up straight, not all over the place, lad. You're making a right pig's ear of that,' the foreman balled, and started to walk away.

'Dick Head.' muttered the young man.

'What did you just say?' asked the foreman.

Startled, the apprentice quickly replied, 'I said, this glue is making me feel sick in the head.'

The foreman carried on with his tour, shaking his head. 'I don't know, young 'uns today,' he mumbled to himself.


The Colliery Manager Bill Sankey and his team were carrying out a last-minute inspection of the arrangements and when Robert Kilpatrick saw Elizabeth Hardy he left the group and walked across to her. With the press and TV reporters surrounding her, he cheerfully addressed her, 'Ah, good morning, Miss Hardy. How are the arrangements going?'

The pressmen all turned to look at the tall, well-dressed man who had spoken to her.

'Oh, fine, Mr Kilpatrick. I was just briefing these gentlemen of the press about the arrangements, and the fact that the London train is running an hour late, but otherwise the arrangements are well in hand.'

'Good, I will leave you to it then,' and he re-joined the management group.


The train pulled into Wigan station seventy minutes late due to the Prime Minister having a television interview with the BBC in London that had overrun.

Outside the station a large crowd had gathered, including a few local journalists, along with a number of police officers, and the Mayor of Wigan, in his full regalia, waiting to greet the VIPs. The public in the crowd were mainly women.

The Prime Minister's luxury Bentley had been driven from London earlier by his driver, and headed a line of luxury limousines hired from a local firm.

As the party emerged from the station they were greeted by a loud booing from the crowd — a response to the Tories' current energy policy which was very unpopular in the Lancashire area.

Stepping forward, the Mayor held out his hand towards the Prime Minister, 'Welcome to Wigan, Prime Minister' the mayor said and the Prime Minister shook his hand. At that moment Wigan's Silver Band struck up with Barnet and Siebert's 'March of the Cobblers .'

The police quickly formed a tunnel and led the Prime Minister and the VIPs to their waiting Limousines and the cars immediately set off for Redman's Colliery.


Ivy, hands on hips, stood looking at the tables laden with food for the visitors. With her canteen ladies she had been busy all morning preparing and then setting out the display they were now admiring in the manager's conference room.

'Right, Jenny, tick things off that list while me and Sheila check what's laid out here.'

'What shall I do, Ivy?' asked Peggy.

'Peggy, you and Jane go back to canteen and bring over the squash drinks we made earlier. And get them lads in yard to carry over those crates of pop.

'Eey, Jenny, I like the way you've cut those sandwiches like a triangle; looks really posh.'

'Aye, Ivy, I saw them in Gorners café last week, and thought by gum, them look nice.'

'Okay, we'll start with sandwiches. Tick 'em off as I shout them out: Smoked salmon, chicken, tongue, ham, cheese, egg and cress.'

'Now open rolls: tuna, chicken, egg and cress and smoked salmon.'

'Now for the other stuff: cheese and pineapple on sticks, salad, chicken legs, coleslaw, miniature pork pies, mini sausage rolls, mushroom and ham volley thingy's.'

'Now puddings: trifle, egg custards, fruit tarts, individual cream cakes, cream horns, and finally cheese and biscuits.'

'All present and correct, Sir.'

'You daft bugger. Sheila. But I must admit they do look like soldiers lined up like that. Do you think there's enough?'

'Of course there is, Ivy, plenty. Let's cover then up with these paper towels.'

Just then the door opened and in walked Bill Sankey.

'Wow, Ivy. What a spread. It's not royalty that's coming, only politicians.'

'I know, but we want to show the southern toffs what we up north can do.'

'Well you have certainty done that. Well done, and thank you girls,'


After a four-mile drive, the leading two police motorcycle escort riders turned down the narrow lane that led to the Redman's Colliery.

Lined up to welcome them at the colliery car park were the manager, in plastercast, and his team.

The convoy drew up alongside the management team and the driver jumped out to open the limousine's door for the Prime Minister.

'Good morning, Prime Minster. I am Bill Sankey. the Colliery Manager. Welcome to Redman's Colliery.'

The press and TV reporters were standing a few feet away, and one of the shouted, 'Prime Minister, why are you visiting a coalmine in Lancashire?'

The Prime Minister hesitated for a moment and turning to the Manager said, 'Excuse me a moment, Mr Sankey.'

He then confidently strolled over to the reporters and stopped in front of them. A well-known BBC news reporter held a microphone in front of the Prime Minister, saying 'Prime Minister, can you tell our viewers the reason behind this visit to Redman's Colliery today?'

Smiling at the camera, the Prime Minister confidently replied, 'The main purpose of this visit, by myself and some of my cabinet, is to see for ourselves how coal is won and to better understand the conditions in which our hard-working miners toil.'

'In addition, it is to show to the opposition party, that contrary to their recent statement, we are not anti-coal, but we the Conservative party believe in a balanced energy policy which allows for new fuels. But we also believe that coal is still the major source of energy in Great Britain. Thank you.'

As the press shouted more questions he turned on his heel and returned to the welcoming party.

Bill Sankey, indicating the entrance to the manager's conference room, said, 'This way gentleman, we have arranged a buffet lunch, during which I will brief you on today's underground visit.'

They all filed into the conference room and Ivy and her girls guided the visitors around the buffet, and the guests filled their plates with a selection of food.

Bill Sankey hobbled to the end of the room, saying,

'Right, gentlemen, sorry I cannot accompany you today because of this recent injury,' he said, tapping his plastercast leg. 'However my undermanger, Tommy Green, will be taking you and guiding you on the underground part of your visit. Now carry on eating, and Frank here will come to each of you in turn. If you will give him your sizes — boots, waist, chest etc. — he can then prepare your underground clothing, which will then be ready laid out for you when we are ready to go down.'

'One thing I should warn you is that matches, lighters cigarettes, cigars — in fact anything pertaining to smoking — are banned underground, classed as contraband. So please ensure that you have none of these items about your person as you prepare to go underground. It is a legal requirement, under the Coalmines Act, that every person is physically searched for such items before going down a coal mine.'

'Enjoy your lunch. Ivy and her ladies will look after you and I will see you all later.'

As he moved to leave, one of the visiting party approached him saying, 'Excuse me, Mr.Sankey, could I please have a quiet word, in private please?'

Bill Sankey looked the man up and down and saw a tall, well-built, handsome and fit-looking young man. He could sense that the man had an urgent problem, so smiling he replied, 'Certainly, come into my office.' They stepped the short distance from the conference room to the manager's office.

'Sit down, please. Now, what can I do for you?'

'My name's Drew Martin, Mr Sankey, and I am the Prime Minister's personal bodyguard,'

'Pleased to meet you, Drew.I am Bill. You must have a very interesting job, Drew.'

'Yes, it is, but the thing is you see, as part of my duties I carry a firearm, which I have concealed in a holster beneath my coat.' He pulled his coat to one side, revealing a pistol housed in a tan leather holster.

'From what you have just said, I suspect that you would not want me to take such an item underground?'

Bill's eyes widened, 'Good God! No, Drew, no way.'

'OK, then have you got a safe in your office?'

'Yes, it's over there, and only myself and my Chief Administrator have access to it.'

'That's great. So if it's okay with you, I will place my weapon, unloaded with the ammunition, in your safe whilst I am underground. You must ensure that no one has access to it.'

'Excellent, and I will inform my Admin chap about it and we will keep quiet about this. Let's do it now then it's done with.'

With that, he extracted the key from his pocket, opened the safe and Drew deposited the gun and ammunition and the safe was locked.

# Fifteen

Billy had been working at the pit bottom area for two weeks and on the day of the VIPs' visit, was instructed by the pit bottom Deputy, Charlie Wood, to load the empty materials carts with three-foot wooden chocks, ready for transportation to the far end coalface later in the day.

At about eleven o'clock, after Billy had just enjoyed his Mum's sandwiches and her usual homemade cake, he was approached by Charlie who said, 'Listen, Billy. A party of VIPs is coming on a visit in ten minutes and I want you to follow them at a discreet distance carrying these two steel water cans in case they need a drink.'

'What's VIPs, Mr Wood?' asked Billy.

'Now, lad, VIPs are very important persons and way above the likes of me and thee, so keep thi mouth shut and only speak when spoken to.'

So, as instructed, Billy sat in the shadows near the pit shaft, waiting for the visitors to arrive, but he couldn't resist having a peep into one of the cans. On raising the lid he saw that it had been filled to the brim with crystal clear drinking-water and ice cubes had been added which were now bobbing up and down in the water.

Clean drinking-water was important in the mines. The water running in the pipes to the coalfaces was only used for fire-fighting and dust suppression; it was yellow and acrid, having been pumped from the water lodged in the old workings to keep the current working area safe and dry. It was therefore undrinkable.

Billy quickly replaced the can lid when he heard the noise of the cage approaching and slipped back into the shadows.

The VIP party left the cage led by Tommy the undermanager, who said, 'This way, Gentlemen. Please mind your heads on the gate,' as they stooped out of the cage to stand at the side of the roadway.

When they were all assembled Tommy did a quick head check and led the party down the main roadway towards the far end coalface.

Billy came out of the shadows and followed behind at a distance of about fifty yards.

He followed the party for over an hour and he could see they were nearing their final destination. He made himself scarce and sat down in a roadside manhole ensuring the water cans were safely stowed.

He had been there for quite a while and was thinking, it hadn't been such a bad day. He'd enjoyed his Mum's butties and it's not long to go until finishing time, he thought. He also wondered how his mate Brian was getting along. His thoughts were suddenly interrupted by an almighty blast.

Billy was totally deafened. The blast was immediately followed by a dense cloud of black coaldust which got in his eyes and throat, making him cough and splutter and gasp for breath.

Shaking with fear, his eyes stinging and feeling as though he had gone completely deaf, he shouted out, 'Mam!

Mam! Please help me. God! God! Please, please don't let me die down pit, like me grandad,' as he bust into a fit of uncontrollable tears.

Tommy and the VIP party were standing about twenty yards from the coalface when the explosion occurred.

Tommy was explaining how the tunnellers erected the three-section arch girders which formed the main intake roadway, when he suddenly felt a slight change in the air pressure. He immediately stopped talking and held his head to one side.

In the next moment there was an ear-piercing hiss, and then they all felt a blast of hot air and a massive pressure wave, followed by a loud, violent noise.

A fiery ball of orange flame rushed out from the coalface, followed by a blinding flash.

It lasted only about ten seconds, but to the group it felt like ten minutes.

The Prime Minister, Charles Thornton, was blown off his feet and flung backwards like a rag doll, landing fifteen yards away, smashing his head against a steel roadway arched girder and rendering him unconscious.

Sir Alfred Kenyon, the Coal Board's Deputy Chairman, had been lifted into the air and also hurled backwards against the sidewall of the tunnel. He lay in a crumpled heap at the side of the roadway.

A huge cloud of black coldest descended and almost choked them. A low rumble was heard in the distance, gradually becoming louder and louder until a massive fall of rocks and stones fell crashing to the ground about a hundred yards outwards toward the pit bottom.

The rest of the visiting group were spread out in a

random heap along the main gate roadway.

After a few minutes a strange still silence fell, the only sound being the screams, cries and moans of the injured men.

On feeling the increase in air pressure, Tommy had stopped talking, before he'd experienced an ear-splitting thump that shook the roadway.

He was hit in the chest by the blast of the explosion, and it felt like a massive fist had hit him. He was flung backwards into the air, landing in a heap against the main gate switchgear. He then felt a wave of scorching heat, and he was sure he was going to die.

Tommy lay where he was for a few seconds gathering his thoughts. That's a massive explosion of methane he thought. 'Come on now, am I okay?' Then, slowly, he mentally assessed his body and was relieved to find both his arms and legs appeared to be unharmed. Apart from numerous scratches on his face and arms, a splitting headache and a constant ringing noise in his ears, he was okay. He shook his head, cleared his mind and thanked God he was alive. After a few minutes he slowly rose from the rubble, replaced his helmet and dusted himself down. Tommy then rubbed his aching back and stretched out his arms to ease his sore limbs.

He now realised that it was a major emergency and he must get immediate help. He hobbled over to the wall-mounted telephone about twenty yards from the coalface. Lifting the single earpiece from its brass hook, he placed it against his ear, then sharply turned the handle several times. This action sent a ringing signal to the pit bottom office two miles away. Not realising that he was shouting at the top of his voice, because of temporary deafness from the explosive blast, he bellowed, 'Hello. Tommy here. What the bloody hell's happened?'

The phone was answered in the office by young Jimmy Barlow, the underground office lad.

'Hello! Tommy Thunder. Jimmy Barlow here.'

'I'll give thi Tommy Thunder!' shouted Tommy.

'Oh! Sorry, I mean Mr Green.'

'Cheeky sod! what the hell's going on'

'Well, Mr Green, there's been an explosion in the return gate, on the other side of the face from where you are, and it's all a bit confused at the moment. Are you alright?'

'No, you lippy bugger, we are not alright. I've got the British Prime Minister, half his cabinet and Sir Alfred Kenyon from the Coal Board scattered all over the place. God knows what state they are in. Get off thee arse and get Mr Sankey the Manager to organise things and ring me back pronto.' He slammed the ear-piece back on its hook and headed off to investigate the situation.

First he examined the Prime Minister, who was now coming round but appeared to be confused. He was now breathing steadily.

As a trained First Aider, Tommy carefully carried out a systematic examination of the Prime Minister. He first noticed a large cut to his cheek, which was bleeding freely. He quickly removed the red first-aid tin off his belt and took out a sterile pad dressing. After he'd applied it to the PM's cheek, strapping it in place with the bandage tails, the bleeding quickly reduced.

The Prime Minister muttered a confused thank you and then Tommy positioned him in the recovery position, telling him to relax and breathe slowly while he treated the rest of the party.

As he moved from a kneeling position he was surprised to see at his side the Prime Minister's security guard.

'Tommy, I'm Drew Martin. I've been trained as an Army Medic. I'll help you treat the injured.'

'Well thank God something's gone right today. I'd be really grateful for that. But Drew, th'ys not got a scratch on thee, how did you manage that, lad.'

'Well, Tommy, I've spent many years in the Army and in some very tricky areas where sudden explosions have happened, usually caused by the enemy trying to blow us up. Somehow, one develops a sort of sixth sense when it's going to happen. That slight change in air pressure caused me to react in an instinctive way. Without further thought I automatically flung myself onto the floor, rolling into a tight ball with my arms wrapped tightly around my head. Hence I was protected from the blast and flying debris.'

'I too felt the pressure change a bit,' said Tommy, 'but I had no idea what was going to happen and was totally unprepared. Well done, lad. Now come on, Drew, let's have a look at this lot.'

As they approached Sir Alfred Kenyon they saw to their horror a large jagged bone sticking out of his left calf. The Deputy Chairman was completely unconscious but breathing freely.

'Shit,' Tommy muttered. 'That's a bad complicated fracture.'

Again, from his first-aid tin, he carefully removed two large sterile dressings and gently positioned them around the bone and the open wound, to protect the fracture. Finally he covered the whole area with a triangular bandage.

'Good work, Tommy,' said Drew. 'But if he regains consciousness he may try to move his leg and do untold damage to it. We;d better try to immobilise it.'

'OK, Drew, follow me,' said Tommy, and he led Drew back

towards the coalface, where a large bright-red First Aid tube was hanging from the steel roadway rings. These tubes were about eight feet long and contained stretchers and splints at one end and at the other a large square box with numerous additional first-aid supplies. He opened the end flaps and selected four wooden splints. From the box he extracted several triangular bandages.

'Wow, Tommy, I thought the Army was well equipped! Does every pit have this equipment?'

'Not only every pit, Drew, but you'll find these first-aid tubes in every single coalface in both the intake and return roadways.'

'Well I take my hat off to your organisation.'

They then returned to their casualty, carrying the equipment between them. This time Drew took charge and placed the splints either side of the fracture and carefully bandaged them in place above and below the injury with triangular bandages. As he was doing this the Deputy Chairman cried out in pain, then fell back into unconsciousness.

'OK, Drew, that's a neat job. Now if he later regains consciousness he may be in great pain and I will have to give him a shot of morphine.'

'Did you say morphine?' said Drew with amazement in his voice.

'Aye, lad, why?'

'Do you mean you have a supply of morphine down here?'

'Of course, lad. Every mine has.See that concrete block hanging up near that red first-aid box we've just used?' Tommy pointed back towards it.

Drew looked back to where Tommy was pointing and saw a square concrete block, about two foot square, hanging from two chains bolted to the girder near the tube.

'Well morphine, in all mines, is stored securely in a small metal safe that is built into that square concrete block you see. Only specially trained first-aiders, such as me, are allowed to carry a key to these safes. In them are phials of morphine, swabs and labels. But they can only be used in serious first-aid emergencies,' explained Tommy.

'See, I have my morphine key on a string around my neck.'

'Unbelievable! What planning. As a Medic in the army I carried two ampules of morphine around my neck, and in battle every soldier had the same. But why down a mine, Tommy, it doesn't make sense?'

Tommy paused and looked Drew in the eyes. 'Drew, tell me, why did you have those ampules of morphine around your neck?'

'Well obviously, we were usually in the middle of nowhere miles from any hospital.'

'And where are you now, Drew?'

'Bloody hell, Tommy! Of course! God, I now know you miners are as much at risk down here as any soldier. My respect for miners has just gone up a lot. OK, let's get stuck in again.'

Drew then turned the patient's head to one side to ensure that if he were sick, he would not choke on his own vomit.

'There, that's the best we can do for him now,' Drew said.

Much to their relief they found that the rest of the VIPs were only suffering from minor cuts and bruises. They were all confused and dizzy and  some of them groaned constantly.

'Listen up, everyone,' Tommy shouted, to get their attention.

'There's been an explosion. I've sent word to the surface and they will organise something and ring me back. You are all safe for now. The Prime Minister is okay but the Deputy Chairman is unconscious and has a broken leg which me and Drew here have treated. He's breathing freely so he's as good as he can be for now. There is some ventilation in here and I am now going to do some tests for firedamp and examine the roadway to see if there's an escape route. We can't go via the coalface because there will have been a roof fall and a good chance of afterdamp gas which is poisonous. So all stay calm, shut up and let me get on with my duties. I will keep you posted. Now all turn your cap-lamps off except one; we must conserve what we've got.'

'Drew, stay here and look after them. I will do an inspection and see you in a bit.'

Tommy then walked a few yards away and lowered the flame on his flame safety lamp, to the small testing bubble. He switched off his cap-lamp and held his lamp up to eye level.

Only in one place could he see the trace of a white ghost-shape, just on top of the blue testing flame, and it was not a complete triangle. He knew this represented about one and a half per cent firedamp in the air and he considered it acceptable in this situation.

Walking out he examined the state of the roof, testing it by using his undermanager's travelling stick.

Things looked reasonably okay until he was about a hundred and fifty yards out, when he met with a solid wall of stone and rock — a major fall brought about by the explosion.

Scowling, he sat down to gather his thoughts and mopped his brow.

After a few minutes, he thought he heard a faint sobbing. He listened carefully and again noticed it, coming from a manhole at the side of the roadway.

These manholes were like sentry style boxes, dug into the rock at the side of the roadway. They were about six feet tall by a yard wide, made as a safety refuge for if and when material carts were being transported to the coalface. If any of the tubs should break free, the manholes were a place of escape.

Following the sound, he peered into the manhole and found a small young lad with a tear-stained face covered jet-black with coaldust. Sobbing his heart out, the lad looked up at Tommy with startled white eyes.

'Nay, lad, what's tha doing there?' said Tommy, kindly.

'Oh it's Mr Green.' Billy squeakily replied in a relieved voice. 'I'm Billy, and it's only my second week down pit. Mr Woods, the pit bottom deputy, gave me the job as water carrier in case the VIPs needed a drink. I was having a rest in here when this massive big bang occurred followed by a big dust cloud. What's happened Mr Green. I'm really scared.'

'Hello. Billy. Now what's your last name?'

'Jones, Mr Green.'

'Tha dad's not Johnny Jones, by any chance is he, Billy?'

'Aye, Mr Green. Do you know him?'

'Do I know him lad! I'll say so. Me and thee dad are old mates. We were in the Boys Brigade together as young lads.'

'Well it's okay lad, thy safe here, and Billy, now there's been an explosion in return gate I'm afraid we're stuck here for a bit. But stay with me and thy will be okay. Are them thi water bottles there lad?' said Tommy, in a calm, friendly way.

'Yes, Mr Green,' said Billy, 'I put them at the back of the manhole when I came in and they have survived alright. Do you want a drink?'

'Well done, Billy,' he replied. 'Good lad, we will need them. They'll come in handy, and no, I don't need a drink for now. But thanks for asking.'

'Billy I know it's only your second week, but today I want you to become a man. I am appointing you as my special Number One Assistant during this emergency. OK?' He patted Billy on his back.

'Oh, thanks, Mr Green," replied Billy.'I'll not let you down. What do you want me to do?'

'Well, grab those two water cans and follow me. And remember, as you are now my brave assistant you have to stay calm and do as I say. Right, follow me.' As he walked back, Billy's little frame followed behind the bulk of Tommy, carrying his precious cargo of water bottles, back towards the injured VIPs.

## *Sixteen*

The shaker pans suddenly stopped and a strange peace and quiet descended on the coalface.

The colliers knew this meant only one thing. It was ten o'clock and meal break time, known officially as snap time, although the men had their own local slang name for it, which was 'jack-bit time'.

The men left the coalface and climbed down into the main gate area to retrieve their snap tins, a necessity to prevent the mice, ever present in the mine, from eating their food.

Along with their water bottles they gathered as a group and squatted in the typical miners' pose — on their haunches — to eat their sandwiches.

'Bloody spam again, I'll kill her!' cried Horace Brown. 'She knows I don't like it. That's to get her own back as we had a big row last night because she wouldn't let me get me leg over. What's thy got Roundall?'

'Me?' replied Roundall, 'Me Mam looks after me proper. She's put up my favourite, corned beef with Barton's sliced beetroot. He opened his tin to reveal slices of thick Warburton's bread, the outside stained with the tell-tale sign of the leaking beetroot juice. Aye, she's good, me Mam, and look, she's even added a thick slice of me favourite Soreen malt loaf, God bless her,'

'Lucky sod,' muttered Horace.

Suddenly a strong smell of raw onion filled the air, as Ivan the Pole bit into a large raw onion, eating it like a ripe apple.

'Bloody hell,' cried Horace. 'I don't know how you can eat onions like that, it's barbaric.'

'It good. In Poland it make strong men,' answered Ivan.

'That's reet, thy knows,' remarked Big George. 'Them Poles are all big lads. Do you know that when they came over here, when the Germans invaded Poland at the start of the War, like Ivan here, a lot of them came to work down pit, but a lot went on to become Spitfire pilots and thankfully helped Britain to win the war. So don't be calling Poles, Horace. We owe them a lot.'

'Horace,' added Alan Pryce, in his singy Welsh accent. 'You know, you should never go to sleep after having a big row with your wife; you should always make up, as you never know what will happen next day and you may live to regret those last angry words.'

'That's true,' chipped-in Gig George.

'Ernie Walker, the NUM Branch Union Secretary, always said, 'always make friends with thi wife at bed time', and it was rumoured that he had a large sign over his bedhead saying,'All Disputes Settled Here'.

Laughing, Horace added, 'Ah but he was a silly sod, and a lazy bugger. I remember, when he worked down pit, he had the smallest shovel in pit and biggest spoon in canteen. He was also as thick as pig shit. When he first became the Union man, he was once asked, by a collier, what a cubic foot was, and he replied, I don't know, but put a compensation claim in and Union will get thi some money for it.'

They all burst out laughing and Roundall started to relate a story he had heard at the last rescue-training course.

'The lecturer was telling us that when he was a younger lad, he worked with the pit surveyors. His main job was each week to go underground and measure how many yards the tunnellers had advanced that week. He would measure and log it and when on the surface inform the Manager of the yardage. One day, the Manager told him he should deduct a yard from the week's yardage so that he could pay the miners less. In return he would make sure the lad got an extra £5 in his wages each week, but to keep it to himself. Well, although he didn't like it, he felt he couldn't go against the Manager's wish, and felt he had to go along with it.'

'The following week he took his measurement, and when he got to the tunnel face told the chargehand the reduced yardage, making out that this figure was the true one. The chargehand took him to one side and said, 'Listen, lad. When you measure each week, add a yard and we will give thee a fiver each time, okay?' To which he readily agreed.'

'He told us, with a knowing wink, that for the next three years he got, an extra £10 a week for giving the exact right measurement to both sides.'

They were all still laughing when the main gate conveyor started up, to signify the end of snap time, so they started to return to the coalface.

Just as they stood up, a sudden explosive blast blew from the coalface, knocking them all over. This was followed by a choking mass of coaldust that obliterated the scene.

After a few seconds the only sound to be heard was the men coughing loudly.

'Everyone alright?' shouted Roundall, his eyes steaming and forming rivers in the jet-black of his covered face.

Slowly, the men began to respond.

Roundall, being a part-time rescue man, had regularly attended training and exercises with the full-time Mines Rescue Brigade. So he knew instinctively what had happened and what action to take.

'Right, lads,' he said, 'That's an explosion of methane. Time to get out of here, quickly. Can everybody walk?'

Gathering all the men in a group, Roundall lead them away from the coalface towards the pit bottom.

When they got to the pit bottom they found chaos, with men shouting and the phones ringing continuously.

Charlie Wood, the deputy, had taken charge and was sending the men up the shaft in the cage as they arrived at the pit bottom.

'Roundall, thank God thee and the men are okay. Get up to the surface straight away and report to the Manager's Office. No doubt they will be needing all part-time rescue men such as thi'self.'

With that, Roundall's team entered the cage and Charlie told the onsetter to signal it away.

As the cage slowly came to surface level, the men saw a hive of activity. Vans and lorries were driving back and forth and clusters of surface workers were receiving orders from the surface foreman.

They left the cage and Roundall made his way to the Manager's Office. His men walked to the canteen where they would wait to see if they were needed in any rescue attempt.

# *Seventeen*

Earlier, Charlie Wood, the pit bottom deputy, was in the return airway when he felt the air pause, then continue, after which a cloud of choking dust overwhelmed him. He staggered to the air doors, groping his way forward.

On reaching the doors he quickly pulled the first door open and went through the other two doors to the main intake pit bottom roadway.

Rubbing his eyes with his handkerchief he quickly ran and burst into the pit bottom office, just as the office clerk, Jimmy Barlow, was on the telephone.

A few moments earlier, the Colliery Administration Officer, Robert Kilpatrick, had answered the ringing telephone on his desk. 'Robert Kilpatrick here,' he said calmly, as an excited and nervous voice on the other end said, 'Hello, Mr Kilpatrick, this is Jimmy Barlow here at the pit bottom office. I've just had a call from the Undermanager. Have you heard about the explosion and the falls in the roadways?'

'Yes, Jimmy. The Manager is quite aware of the situation and has things in hand,' replied Robert.

'Sorry, Mr Kilpatrick, just checking. Well the

Undermanager has ordered me to ring you and ask that Mr Sankey ring him to give him an update on the rescue plans as they develop.'

'OK, Jimmy, leave it to us, but make sure that you switch the telephone system through so that Mr Sankey can ring Mr Green direct. Is Charlie Wood around?'

'Yes, Sir, he's just come in, I'll put him on,' he said as he handed the pit bottom deputy the telephone, saying, 'Mr Kilpatrick wants a word with thee.'

'Charlie, can you make sure that any men that come to the pit bottom are sent up to the surface straight away, and no one is to go inbye until the rescue men give permission?'

'It's a bad do, this. Okay, I'll do that, Mr Kilpatrick.'

'Okay, Charlie, and thank you and goodbye,' replied Mr Kilpatrick.

Robert knocked on the Manager's adjoining door and after receiving an acknowledgement to enter he briefed the Manager on the phone call.

The Manager later rang Tommy who answered straightaway.

'Hello, Mr Sankey. What's happening?' said Tommy, not needing to wait for confirmation of who was on the other end of the telephone.

'Right, Tommy,'replied the Manager. 'And from now on my name's Bill, forget the formalities. First, give me your assessment of the current situation where you are.'

'Well,' said Tommy. 'First, the Deputy Coal Board Chairman, Alf Kenyon, has a bad complicated fracture which I have immobilised. He is unconscious, but breathing, so I have put him in the recovery position. I could do with a chat to Nurse Belshaw for advice on this one. I may have to administer morphine if he's in great pain when he recovers consciousness If you could arrange that please? The rest have minor injuries, the worst being the Prime Minister who has a bad gash on his face, which I have treated. He's a bit confused, and concerned, but he is becoming stronger as time goes by. I have a young lad here who was the water carrier for the VIPs so we have a good supply of good clean water. I've carried out a detailed inspection, and I reckon the fall in the main roadway is about a hundred and fifty yards, but it's solid with loose material. I've not been on the coalface, in case there's a build up of gas, and I guess that it is completely blocked. There is a flow of fresh air getting through. I've tested for gas and it's at an acceptable level of one and a half per cent, so we are okay for the moment. Oh, and Bill, you know Drew, the PM's bodyguard? Well although he is a policeman with the protection squad, in a previous life he was a trained medic and he certainly knows his stuff. He's been a great help to me, taking some of the pressure off, I can tell you. Good news at last.'

'Well done, Tommy. As always, the true professional. Now from my part, I have had an inspection carried out on the other side of the fall from you, by the chief Mines Inspector and a full Mines Rescue Team, including our part-time lads. You are right in thinking the fall is about a hundred and fifty yards long, and unfortunately consists of large rocks and small, loose material that is packed solid. It's going to be a bit tricky trying to dig through. The rescue team have had a go but have had to stop as it's too loose to shore up. The coalface side is completely blocked so there is no way we can get through to you that way. We are having a surface crisis meeting in about twenty minutes where all active parties will get together to produce an action plan. I am going to use all of our part-time rescue men. I know the Mines Rescue Team are good but I may need some more muscle to help with any excavation. I have also asked Dan, the Foreman Blacksmith, to come along, as he is good at applying logic and ideas to tricky situations.

Dan is a good man to have beside you in situations like this.'

'Aye I know Dan's abilities well, and am glad he is included,' replied Tommy.

'Well,' continued the manager, 'when we have a detailed plan I will come back to you with an update. In the meantime you keep everyone calm and keep monitoring the atmosphere. Okay?'

'Right, Bill,' said Tommy. 'One other thing, though. The PM is worried about who is running the country whilst he is trapped down here.'

'Oh,' replied the manager. 'Tell him to forget all about that, as the Deputy PM and the rest of his Cabinet have taken charge, and are now at a meeting at 10 Downing street and are dealing with any national or international events, and fortunately there are no major problems. The biggest crisis is here at Redman's. The media has gone crazy and the pit is under siege, surrounded by the world's press, TV and radio personnel and equipment. Ivy is making a fortune in the canteen.'

'Eey, Bill, I could murder one of Ivy's meat pies and a cup of sweet tea at the moment,' said Tommy.

'Well, Tommy, nothing would give me greater pleasure. I will make sure that when we complete the rescue you have as many of Ivy's pies as you can eat.'

'Thanks, Mr Sankey, oh sorry, Bill. I'd better go and check how things are and give them an update.' With that they both hung up their telephones.


Bill Sankey sat at his desk reflecting on how lucky he was to have an Undermanager as strong and powerful as Tommy controlling the situation in the trapped area.

Twenty minutes later, in a crowed conference room, all the colliery management were assembled, including Dan, the Foreman Blacksmith, Annie Belshaw, the Colliery Nurse, the Chief Mines Inspector Mr Antony Royle, along with Captain Stead the Area General Manager. The rescue team assembled around the conference table.

As there were so many in the room some had to stand behind the chairs. Spread out on the conference table were plans of the mine and detailed drawings showing the area of the explosion.

Mr Sankey addressed the gathering, 'Right everyone, I have had Frank Taylor here draw up the plans and produce overhead transparencies of the situation. He is fully up to date and will now brief you. Okay, Frank, away you go.'

Frank coughed nervously, switched on the overhead projector and placed his first slide on the projector. This was a plan of the district, showing the coalface, along with both the intake and return roadways. Frank had drawn in details of the fall area and the position of the seat of the explosion. He had also listed the names of all the trapped personnel.

He explained that the explosion had occurred about a third of the way along the coalface and was probably caused by an electrical fault, as one had been causing problems and had been reported earlier in the shift. He went on to say how lucky they had been in that the explosion had occurred just after snap time, when all the men were returning to the coalface after having had their meal break.

Frank stated that the Undermanager had reported to Mr Sankey that there was at present a flow of air and little gas, but that the Deputy Coal Board Chairman was unconscious but the rest of the party had only slight injuries, however, the Prime Minister had a bad cut to his face and was a bit confused.

'What's new in that?' muttered Jimmy Smith, the NUM miners' representative.

Ignoring this comment, Frank continued to say that they had a rescue team, along with the Ventilation Officer, at the scene, and that they were monitoring this side of the fall area. He then switched off the projector and handed back to the Colliery Manager.

'Right, thanks for that Frank. Any comments?' asked Bill Sankey.

'Well, the main problem, as I see it,' began Mr Antony Royle, the Chief Mines Inspector, 'is the extraction and support of the loose material in order to construct an escape route.'

'Yes, I agree with that,' said Bill.

The manager then asked Captain Stead if had anything to add.

'No, Mr Sankey, you seem to have everything covered. Just say if you need me to bring any of the Area's facilities into play.'

'Thank you, Captain, I am glad you mentioned that. Can you please arrange for the Coal Board's Mobile Laboratory and its staff to be positioned in the yard, so that they can analyse any air samples straightaway, as they come up the pit? And also the Area's mobile First Aid cabins?'

'Leave that to me, Mr Sankey,' replied Captain Stead.

'Right,' Bill continued, 'A lot of you know Dan, our Foreman Blacksmith here, and how in the past he has come up with ingenious solutions to difficult situations, so I have asked him to attend this meeting to see if he can help, although we have never had a problem as difficult as this in the past. Dan, any thoughts?'

All eyes turned to Dan, who sat at the conference table calmly and quietly smoking his beloved full-strength.

After a few seconds Dan wiped his hand over his greying full head of hair, took off his black-rimmed spectacles and thoughtfully replied, 'I've a germ of an idea, but I don't want to build your hopes up too much until I have had a chat with my blacksmith team back in the workshop to see if they think it will work. So, Mr Sankey, I'll get back now if that's okay, and start planning. Then I will let you know straightaway.'

'Okay, Dan. Off you go and tell your lads how vital this is for us.'

Dan then left the meeting.

'Now,' continued the Manager, 'I want the rescue team to organise a relief team to take over from the present team and also produce a twenty-four hour rota so the area is continually manned. Frank, I want you, along with Mr Kilpatrick, to produce a press release giving an update. Oh, and better not to say too much about the PM. I think I had better approve any release before it goes out.'

'Ivy, I want you and your girls to see that everyone is fed and watered. In addition, Ivy, can you send some food down to the men working at the rescue site? Frank Taylor will help you to arrange the transport of that.'

'Okay, Mr Sankey,' said Ivy. 'My girls and I are keen to help in any way we can. We have even arranged sleeping arrangements in the kitchen for us to provide twenty-four hour service These are our lads too, you know,' finished Ivy, in a faltering voice.

The Manager grinned. 'Fantastic, Ivy. That's what I like to hear. The Dunkirk spirit. Frank, make sure the press get to hear about that.'

'Annie, I want the First Aid room fully operational and arrange that the Ambulance and Hospital services are on standby for when the call goes out. And ring Tommy as he wants a word about using morphine.'

'Okay, Mr Sankey, I'll see to that. Just one thing though.

I would like to ask the Chief Mines Inspector for his permission for me to go underground to help with any medical injuries when the men are rescued.'

Antony Royle replied swiftly, 'Well, most of us know that since 1842, under the Mining regulations, women are not allowed to work underground. However, I do have emergency powers to override that, and in this case I am happy to do so, Annie.'

'Thank you, Sir, I really appreciate that,' responded Annie.

'Okay, that's it. I will brief you all later and I will be going down the mine myself in about half an hour. Thank you all for attending,' concluded the Manager.

With that, the meeting broke and everyone went their separate ways to carry out their assigned tasks.

# *Eighteen*

As Tommy approached the group underground, the Prime Minister, Charles Thornton, wearily said, 'Tommy, I see you're organising everything, taking charge in this emergency with a clear, calm and confident attitude. I feel useless. Come and sit by me and tell me how you do it.'

'To be able to answer that, Sir,' Tommy reflected, 'first you have to understand the mining industry and its values and structure. You see, the Colliery Manager is in total control at a pit. To the men he is God.

He is responsible for the whole mine and must ensure it operates safely and efficiently. In addition to producing as much coal as possible to return a maximum profit, he is responsible for both the surface and underground operations. In fact, Prime Minister, at this pit he has more direct power here than you. Even the Police, by law, are not allowed to take any actions underground without the Manager's agreement, and even then he would control any operation. To qualify as a Colliery Manager he must have carried out years of intense mining studies to at least degree level to be awarded The Colliery Managers Qualification — what is officially called a First Class Mining Certificate. On the practical side, he must have worked on every job throughout the mine, especially on a coalface. So, you see, he knows every aspect of the industry, from coalface to the coal lorry. My job as undermanager, as the title suggests, means that I have total control and management of all the underground operations. My job is my life; I have been in mining since leaving school at fifteen, starting at the pit bottom as a haulage lad. I've studied mining at college and gained my Undermanager Certificate, called a Second-class certificate. Over the years, and with experience gained, one gets to know the nature of the mine and can anticipate its moods and changes. With this knowledge and experience you can adapt and respond to the unexpected changes nature throws at you. My wife, Mabel, will tell you how intense I am about the pit. It's my second home, although Mabel would say it's my first home. I live and breathe it. I love it! Miners have a term for this disease — they call it 'pit brunt'. The men I know, behind my back, call me 'Tommy Thunder' because of this. I secretly encourage this because, like a Sergeant Major, a certain amount of fear instils discipline and respect from the men. Only the other day a collier working on the coalface asked me the time. Now the men know I always carry a pocketwatch in my waistcoat on a fob chain.'

Tommy reached into his waistcoat pocket and pulled out his gold pocket watch.

'This gold watch belonged to my Grandad and I treasure it, but last week I had taken it in for cleaning. In my bits drawer I found an old cheap Ingersoll pocketwatch and chain and decided to use that until my gold watch was ready. It turned out to be utterly useless, losing time and was totally unreliable. So when this collier asked me the time, I resisted, and told him to get on with his work. Roundall, the collier, persisted in asking, so, eventually, feigning a rage, I snatched the old watch and chain out of my pocket and threw it into the waste area with all my might and we both heard it smash and tinkle into a thousand pieces. I then said with glarey eyes, "Now no-one knows the time. Get on with thi work." Now I know this story will be passed on by the men; they think I have smashed my best gold watch. Sometimes I see a fear and panic in the men's eyes when I visit their working area, and if for example I find a prop missing on the coalface, I only have to tell them once to correct it and they will scuttle off quickly to obey my order and replace it. So you see, Sir, it's in my blood and I know that despite this behaviour, the men, deep down, trust and fear me and also respect me. However, I do have another side. Take young Billy there, he and lads like him are our future. I will protect him from harm. I know his dad well and he will knows Billy is safe with me. I will be like a mother-hen, looking after all her chicks, protecting all the young lads that come to my pit. Sorry about the lecture, Sir.'

The Prime Minister sat wrapped in thought. He looked Tommy in the eyes and, shaking his head, eventually said, 'Well Tommy, what can I say? I could learn a lot from you. I went to Eton, then I gained a First class honours degree at Oxford University, and now I am trying to run the country, and I don't know a fraction of what you know. Perhaps you should go into politics, Tommy?'

'I don't know about that, Sir, but if you politicians understood the miners' life you may think differently about the industry. The men know mining is hard and dangerous. They work hard and play hard, even though they profess to be glad to get away from the job. In the Miners Welfare Clubs at night and weekends, the talk inevitably turns to life at the pit. Even the old retired miners who are gasping for breath, chatting at the street corner, are usually reminiscing or telling mining stories. When politicians close mines it destroys the miners' lives and decimates the villages. At present there is a fine balance between fossil fuels such as coal, gas, oil and, on a smaller scale, nuclear fuel, and as you are now moving to oil and gas, I feel you are laying down problems for the future. When our oil and gas run out and most of the mines have been closed, and our mining villages and communities have disappeared, then we will be totally reliant on foreign countries that owe no alliance to us. The coal is here, it's ours, and there's plenty of it, and mining operations are now getting more mechanised and safer and easier. Okay, I have said my bit. I apologise again for sounding-off. Now I must get on with organising this rescue, but to be honest it's out of my hands now.'

'Don't apologise, Tommy. That was a lesson in straight talking, from an honest man, who I am beginning to have a great respect for. I will ponder on what you have said, as you have given me an insight on something that we have known about, but chosen to ignore.'

Tommy rose and walked over to Billy.

'Billy, lad, go round and make sure everyone has a drink of water while I find out what's happening on the surface.'

# *Nineteen*

Dan walked across the colliery yard towards his Blacksmiths shop, deep in thought. As he passed the surface compound near to the fitters shop he saw equipment on the floor and a smile came to his face as he thought of something that could just be the job.

He popped his head round the shutter door and saw the foreman fitter working on a conveyor gearbox with three of his fitter mates.

'Hi,' he shouted. 'Have you a minute?'

The foreman left this men and walked over to Dan.

'Hello Dan. Bad do about those VIPs being trapped. I'm no lover of the Tories, but I wouldn't wish this on anybody, and Tommy Thunder's trapped there as well. I've heard they've asked you for ideas. Can we help?'

'Ay, that's what I want to chat to you about. See that apparatus in your surface compound? Is that for the new delivery system at the surface washery?'

'It is, Dan. Why do you ask?'

'Well,' replied Dan. 'I have had an idea and I may need to pinch them from you, if I can design what I have in mind.'

'Dan, take them. If it will help to rescue those poor

trapped men, you have my blessing.'

'Okay, thanks. See you later.'

At the Blacksmiths shop the men were assembled waiting for Dan's return.

'Have you heard about this explosion? Dan's been summoned to a big meeting with all top brass, to see if we can help in any way. He should be on his way back now. Ah, here he is now,' said Freddy, Dan's number one blacksmith, as the Foreman strode through the open shutter door.

'Right, lads, gather round. We've been asked for ideas to help rescue the trapped VIPs.'

The men formed a group around a large metal steel plate on the wall outside Dan's office. This plate was used every day for displaying notices, design ideas or just list of forthcoming jobs. Today it had been wiped clean by Albert, in readiness for this session.

Dan picked up a piece of white chalk and turned to face his men.

'Now according to the Manager, the problem is that the main roadway is completely blocked solid, with a fall that is about 150 yards long. Because it's loose rocks it's too dangerous to try to dig into it, and also they consider it would take too long to drive a road through. So they thought the best bet is to attack it from the coalface, which is also blocked, however with that it's all coal, and the blockage is less, only about 20 yards.'

'But how can we help with that? We're blacksmiths, not colliers,' the pits bit sharpener asked, with a puzzled expression on his face.

Dan put his hands on his hips, and replied, 'I'm coming to that, just give me time. Well, they have tried digging into the coal and it seems there is a big void over the area so that as soon as they dig, fresh coal fills the area they've just

134

excavated. So they now think digging through the blocked roadway is the only solution. I've given it a lot of thought and I have an idea, but I need your input to iron out any problems, so here is my plan. In the surface materials compound there are a number of forty-inch cylindrical tubes made of heavy gauge steel, each fifteen feet long. They've been specially made for the new coal delivery system for the surface washery. I think we can modify these to provide a sort of protective tunnel to shield the rescue workers when they are excavating the coal.'

Dan picked up the chalk and drew a cylinder on the steel plate. He then drew a circle to represent the end view of the tube.

'Now, inside the bottom of the tube we can make a platform across for the full length of the tube. On this we could weld small rails to take a custom-made cart to extract the coal from the tube. The filled cart will be pulled back by a rope.'

'Just like in that prisoner of war film, where they dug a tunnel to escape and had wooden rails,' exclaimed Albert, excitedly. The men all burst out laughing.

'Aye, Albert, something like that,' resumed Dan smiling.

'Now, as I was saying, even better, the platform will have a space underneath it, which will accommodate a four-inch pipe, which could provide ventilation to the tube.'

The other day, Frank Taylor was telling me that they have just taken delivery of a new device, called an air mover, which is a twelve-inch long, four-inch diameter metal tube that has a compressed air supply. It works by discharging the compressed air, inducing air from the surrounding area. Something they called a 'venturi effect'. I thought we could somehow attach this to the four-inch pipe in our tube and it would supply fresh air to the rescuers as they work. Now, we need some way of pushing the tube forward as the coal is extracted.'

Freddy quickly jumped in, saying, 'I know what will do that! I noticed two hand-operated hydraulic rams near the fitters shop the other day. They would just do the job. I'll go and see if they are still there, and if they are, I will ask the fitters whether we can have them.'

'Good idea, Freddie. Go and check when we have finished this session.'

These additions were made to the chalk drawing.

'Now come on, I need more of your thoughts and ideas,' said Dan.

Out of his waistcoat he pulled a packet of full strength cigarettes, extracted one, and lit it with a match. He contently blew a stream of smoke into the air.

The men stood silently looking at the drawing. Scratching his chin another of Dan's men hesitantly said, 'That's clever, Dan. However the rams will need something to lever against when pushing the tube. How about two hydraulic props, like arcos, that will tighten up against the roof and floor?'

Dan added these to the drawing. 'Good thinking. Anything else, lads?

'Aye,' piped up Ralph, another blacksmith. 'They'll also need something to provide lateral resistance when the rams are pushing the tube against the coal. How about adding the stabilising legs from an old set of compressed air drills?'

'Excellent idea, Ralph,' said Dan, adding this to the drawing.

They all stared at the finished drawing and nodded their agreement.

However Albert still looked puzzled. 'I don't know how it's going to work, Dan. Surely the rubble will be solid and the rams won't be strong enough to push the tubes through the solid rubble?'

'Well Albert,' Dan replied, 'there will be a rescue man in the tube at the far end, spading the rubble onto the truck. Thus, by loosening the rubble, the solidness will be released gradually, allowing the rams to move forward slowly, by small amounts.'

'I see, but it's still very contraceptive though,' said Albert.

They all burst out laughing.

'Yes, it is, Albert,' replied Dan smiling kindly.

Freddy returned from the fitters shop and gave Dan a thumbs-up sign. 'Okay, lads, that seems to settle it. Now we are going to work flat out to produce these tubes. We need to add rings for bolt holes at the end of the tubes, to allow them to be coupled together. I reckon we need to produce thirty-two of these tubes to allow for a couple of spares.

We won't stop until the work is complete, even if we have to work through the night, so get on to your wives and tell them the score. I will arrange with Ivy for the canteen to deliver some food to keep us fed and watered. Now off you go and gather all the materials we need and get cracking. I'm off to brief Mr Sankey.'

# Dan's Rescue Tube

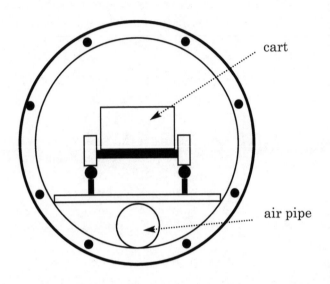

cart

air pipe

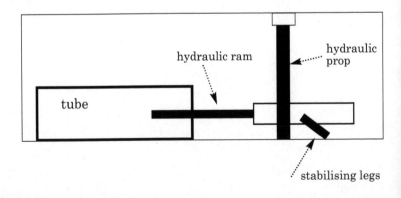

hydraulic ram

hydraulic prop

tube

stabilising legs

# *Twenty*

Tommy picked up the ringing telephone.

'Tommy, Bill Sankey here. How are things going?'

'Well, Bill, I've done another gas test and I reckon there's about one and a half per cent of methane, so I'm reasonably happy with that. There is still enough air filtering through the fall so as far as that goes, things are now calm here. The casualty is still unconscious, his breathing a bit ragged, but I am happy with his condition for the moment. Oh, you know the Prime Minister's body guard, Drew? I can tell you that I am really glad to have someone here to help me who has medical skills.'

'Well, that's good news. But Tommy, we have got a bit of a flap on up here. It seems that we can't locate a young lad called Billy. Charlie Wood sent him after your group with water supplies, but since the explosion we have not been able to locate him. His dad's going spare and threatening to attack the fall himself with his bare hands if need be.'

'Don't fret, Bill. The lad's here with me. Remember me saying I had a lad with fresh water? Well it's Billy Jones, and he managed to escape the explosion as he was resting in a manhole. He even saved his water bottles. He's in good health and tell his dad, Johnny, that I am looking after him. Johnny's an old mate of mine.'

'Right, Tommy, that's a relief. I'll let him know. Now another rescue team are on their way down.'

Dan and his men are constructing what we are calling a rescue tunnel, which consists of strong steel tubes, that will protect the diggers as they dig through the rubble. So I'm coming down to take charge. Take care, Tommy, I will ring later.'

'But Bill, you have a broken leg in plaster!'

'Sod that, Tommy, I can't stop up here whilst this is going on. I'll be okay.'

'Well be careful, Bill. Take your time.'

'Will do. I'll now let Johnny know the good news.'


Ivy picked up the telephone.

'Canteen here,' she said in loud voice.

'Hello Ivy. Colliery Manager here. Is Johnny Jones there?'

'Aye, Mr Sankey, he's here in his dirt with his mates, in a right sad state. He's sat over there now with his head in his hands.'

'Well put him on, Ivy, I've some news that will cheer him up.'

'Johnny!' shouted Ivy. 'Over here. Mr Sankey wants a word with thi. Come round the counter there and take this call.'

Johnny rose slowly and ambled over to the phone with his head held down, expecting bad news. Anxiously, he said, 'Hello, Mr Sankey. Any news yet?'

'He's okay, Johnny! Fit and well, behind the fall and being cared for by Tommy Green.'

Looking up at Ivy and her ladies, Johnny shouted, 'OH THANK GOD! Thank you sir. Tommy's an old mate of mine. I now know Billy's in good hands.'

Ivy, standing near to the counter, with her hands on her hips, suddenly felt tears running down her cheeks. All her girls started to hug each other, laughing.

'Right, Johnny, you go and get bathed and go home and get some sleep. I've enough volunteers and rescue men to deal with this.'

'If it's alright with you, Mr Sankey, I will stay here until it's all over. Thanks for your help.'

'Okay, Johnny. Now put Ivy back on, please.'

Johnny waved Ivy over and handed her the phone.

'Ivy I'm sending some apprentice lads over with some brand new water cans. In two hours' time fill them up with hot, milky, sweet tea and make up a box with twenty hot pies and some sandwiches for the rescue men underground.'

'I will, Mr Sankey, with pleasure. Me and the girls are working through, so let me know when the men need a refill.'

'Smashing Ivy. I am going underground myself in half an hour, so liaise with Mr Kilpatrick, will you?'

'Oh before you go, Mr Sankey, I know you — I bet you've had nowt to eat for ages. Now don't argue with me, I am sending over some boiled ham sandwiches and a flask of tea, so make sure you eat it before you go down pit.'

In his office, Bill Sankey sat, numbed and speechless, as he managed to mutter into the phone, 'Ivy, you're an Angel,' then made a kissing sound as he replaced the phone.

'Bloody hell,' shouted Ivy. 'Manager's just kissed me!'

'Oh, Ivy' gasped Peggy. 'Lucky you, but you've gone bright red.'

'Shut up, Peggy Gornall. Get making his ham butties.'

# Twenty-One

A Coal Board lorry driver was given the task of driving around the village and informing the wives and families of the blacksmiths and welders that their loved ones would not be coming home until the work on the rescue tubes was completed.

Even though they knew food was being supplied, many wives turned up at the blacksmiths shop with sandwiches and flasks.

The blacksmiths shop was a hive of activity, with forges blazing and smiths hammering and shaping the steel rings which would enable the tubes to be connected together to form a continuous steel tunnel.

When a ring was cooled and ready, Albert would take it to the large pedestal drill and drill boltholes into the ring, before it was welded onto the end of a tube.

To save time and speed up the operation, the welders had transported a number of portable welders into the blacksmiths shop from their welding shop across the yard and had set up their own working area at the far end of the blacksmiths shop.

At three o clock in the morning they had completed half

of the tubes when through the side door burst Ivy, Peggy and Nellie dragging a canteen trolley loaded with a large tea urn and a selection of sandwiches and hot pies.

'Ey up, lads, grub's up,' balled Ivy above the industrial noise.

The men, beaming, immediately stopped what they were doing, dropped their tools and rushed over to the trolley.

'Take your time, lads,' Ivy shouted.

'There's plenty to go round. And Albert, I'm sorry, lad, I've not had time to cut the crusts off for you,' joked Ivy.

Albert grinned, feeling pleased to be singled out by Ivy, until Stanley said, 'It's not a compliment, Albert, she's taking the piss.'

'Nay,' said Albert. 'Ivy's alreet, we go back a long way.'

'Come on, lads, tuck in,' encouraged Freddy, and the men took their refreshments and sat on the wooden benches to enjoy their food.

Dan took Ivy to one side, put his hand on her shoulder, and whispered, 'Ivy, you are a star. Thanks a lot, love.'

'Oh, Dan, don't thank me; at this pit we are all a team who pull together in a crisis. Go on, get a pie and some tea before that lot scoff the lot.'


By six o'clock in the morning all the tubes had been welded, holes bored, rails and ventilation tubes fitted and two small-wheeled trucks constructed to run on rails.

Dan called for the men to assemble outside his office.

'Right, lads, well done. You've done a first-class job, but it's not over yet. I want to split you into two teams of six, with one team on the surface at the top of the downcast shaft to sling the tubes under the cage and lower them down the shaft. The second team will be at the pit bottom

144

to receive the tubes and pull them into the main underground roadway. Freddy, you will lead that team and I will lead the surface operations.'

The men nodded their agreement, and discussed among themselves who should be in which team.

Just then, a team of surface workers arrived and proceeded to drag the tubes out into the yard where a Cole's crane was waiting. They attached chains around the tube and the crane slowly lifted it until it was a few feet off the ground. Then the crane crawled towards the downcast shaft, followed by the surface workers.

In line with mining tradition, the Blacksmiths were responsible for the maintenance of the winding equipment, including the cage, its chains and all the wire ropes. They regularly inspected the gear and at scheduled intervals renewed the steel rope, cables and chains. They were used to working closely with the winding-engine men and had special signals to indicate their handling requirements. Over the years the blacksmiths and engine-winders seemed to have developed a telepathic link and seemed to be able to read each other's mind during these delicate operations.

Freddy's team had gone down the mine, and were preparing their equipment as Dan and his team assembled at the shaft's surface level.

Dan briefed the men, and assigned each man his task and duties.

He signalled the engine-man to raise the cage slowly until its base was level with the landing where they were positioned. Signalling the cage to stop, his men then hooked heavy strong chains onto four eyes which were located at the bottom corners of the cage. The eyes were normally used for slinging large items, too big to go in the cage itself, down the mine.

Dan's men then connected the other end of the four chains onto a sling, which had been placed around the first tube.

The men stood clear as Dan signalled for the cage to be raised, very slowly. As the cage started to rise the chain soon tightened and dragged the tube towards the shaft. The men had looped a rope around the end of the tube and, as it left the ground, held it back and let it swing, falling towards the shaft. When the tube was suspended in the centre of the shaft, and steady, the men released the rope and coiled it near to them.

'Right, lads, well done. Let's send it on its way to Freddy.' And Dan signalled for the cage to descend very slowly.

At the pit bottom, Freddy and his team could hear the relay signals and were aware that the first tube was on its way. They started to get ready to receive it. All their cap lamps were focused onto the shaft and a few minutes later the bottom of the tube appeared in view in the glare of their lights.

One of Freddy's men had a long wooden pole which had a steel hook attached to the end, and he leaned forward and hooked the inside end of the tube, pulling it into the roadway. When it was level with the ground, Freddy signalled for the cage to stop. The men took the weight of the tube and the chains were unhooked using the hook and pole. The tube was then dragged onto a haulage cart and taken into the mine by the awaiting haulage hands.

Freddy lowered the cage fully and placed the slinging chains into the cage before signalling it back to the surface at full speed.

'Right, lads. One down, only another thirty-one to go,' said Freddy, laughing.

It took four hours for the blacksmiths to complete the task and they then reassembled at the shop. Mr Sankey, who had returned to the surface, was waiting to congratulate them.

'Right, lads, great job. Now go home and get some well-deserved rest. Dan, can you hang on, please, I want a quick word.'

As the men left, Mr Sankey walked over to Dan.

'Now, Dan, I know it's been a long session, but can you grab some sleep and then go underground in a couple of hours and show the rescue team how the rescue tunnel operates? That's the rams and all that. All the parts should be in place.'

'Aye, Mr Sankey, no problem. Tell you what, I'll have a kip in my office. Send someone over when you want me to go down.'

'Okay, Dan.'

The Manager limped slowly back to his own office.


Dan's office was located near the door of the blacksmiths shop. It was somewhat small, but had a large window facing the work area, where Dan could see all the work activities within the shop. All was quiet now and Dan managed to dose in an old armchair.


A knock on the door woke him up suddenly.

'Yes, come in,' he shouted.

A young surface worker entered the small office.

'Mr Sankey says can you go underground now please.'

'Okay. Thanks, lad. I'll go and get ready, ' answered Dan. He reached into his waistcoat pocket for his full strength cigarettes and matches, opened the packet, extracted a cigarette and lit it with a match. Blowing out the first puff of smoke, he prepared himself for the task ahead. As he walked towards the pit baths he thought about how he would explain the concept of the rescue tube to the underground rescuers.

He arrived at the main intake, where the rescue teams were assembled. Bill Sankey instructed the assembled team to gather round so that Dan could instruct them in the tube system.

# *Twenty-Two*

Number One team were coupled to their breathing apparatus and could therefore not speak. The team captain examined in turn each man's apparatus, and on looking into their face received a thumbs-up to signify that he was okay.

The banksman watched intently as the rescue men prepared to descend the mine for the first inspection.

The banksman signalled for the cage, which rose slowly and came to a halt at the surface level. He than raised the cage gate.

The rescue team leader signalled five hoots on his hooter, and his deputy signalled five in return in a ready acknowledgement.

The team then entered the cage, and the banksman lowered the gate, before slowly lowering them down the mine.

At the pit bottom they slowly and carefully exited the cage and assembled near the office.

The leader studied the mine plan, and then pointed to the roadway that led to the fallen area. Using white chalk he then drew a long arrow on the boards between the roadway girders, and wrote on the names of his team, and the date. He then signalled to the men to move forwards.

Thirty minutes later they reached the fallen area and examined the area in detail. They took air samples before returning to the surface, where they handed them to the staff manning the Area's mobile laboratory.

An hour later, near the site of the fall, the colliery ventilation officer, Ged Winstanley, had arranged for the installation of an auxiliary ventilation fan. This was now whining noisily in the main intake roadway. Connected to the rear of this fan was a thirty-inch flexible tube, that ran for twenty yards, to discharge cold, clean air to the face of the fall.

Although the rescue team's samples had proved negative, the auxiliary air supply was installed as a precautionary measure.

Ged was at the site continually, taking air samples with his methanometer.

His canary was chipping merrily in its cage, hung on a nearby ring arch.


At the site of the fall the rescue team was assembled.

Nurse Annie Belshaw whispered to Roundall, 'Roundall, I really enjoyed our walk on Sunday, but I never thought that the next time I would meet you would be down a coal mine.'

Grinning, Roundall replied, 'I loved our time together and look forward to the next time. But I don't think you should be here, it's too dangerous.'

'Rubbish, I would sooner be here than on the surface, worrying. At least I can attend to any possible injuries here. And besides, I can be with you again.'

Bill Sankey had instructed the assembled team to gather round, as Dan was going to explain the concept of the tube system.

Dan moved to the centre of the roadway and using the Managers travelling stick, pointed to the fallen area.

'Okay, lads, here's the idea. The first tube will be pushed into the face of the fall, and into the rubble as far we can push it. The fitters will then have installed the rams at the rear of the tube. One of you will enter the tube and excavate the rubble at the face of the tube, sending the rubble back by the special mini-tubs inside the tube, which will be pulled back, emptied by the rest of the team, and then returned to the face of the tube. Now I know, it will be very hot in there but, you will see here,' pointing to the pipes, 'we have installed a pipe under the rail track and, at the tube entrance, we will connect an air mover, to this end, which will then blow fresh air and deliver it to the face of the tube where you are working.'

He continued, 'As you excavate and remove the rubble, the powerful rams will gently inch the tube forward into the rubble. These tubes were originally intended as a chute for the surface washery, and have been manufactured from very thick and strong rolled steel, so they will withstand the pressure and weight of the rubble. As progress is made, further tubes and pipes will be bolted on, to give a continuous, safe passage and working area. Now any questions?'

'Well done, Dan,' Roundall commented.

'Bloody brilliant, I say,' said one of the full-time rescue men.

Bill Sankey suddenly jumped up and interrupted with, 'Right then, let's make a start and get these men out.'

The team leader informed his team that because of the clear air, they would not need their breathing apparatus.

The men manhandled the first tube into place right up

to the fall and the fitters connected the hydraulic rams to the tube and operated them to push the tube tight against the rockface.

The first man then scrambled into the tube with his spade and pick.


In the rearranged conference room, Robert Kilpatrick, Elizabeth Hardy and David Thomas, representing the Government, sat behind a desk on which several microphones had been arranged.

Behind them a large notice board was covered with a black cloth, and to its right, a large white projection screen.

In front of them, in rows of chairs, sat the world's press and, positioned in the right-hand corner was a BBC TV camera, mounted on its swivel base.

The noise in the room was so loud that when Robert started to speak no-one could hear him. He banged on the table with a piece of wood and the noise quickly subsided.

'Right, QUIET! Please can we have some order and get this conference started?'

'I am Robert Kilpatrick, Chief Administration Officer for Redman's Colliery, and on my left, most of you know, is Miss Elizabeth Hardy, who is the National Coal Board's Head of Public Relations. On her left is Mr David Thomas, here to represent the Government.'

The room suddenly was ablaze with flashes, as the photographers shuffled and pushed as they vied to get the best shots. Some even climbed little ladders they had brought, to get a better view from the back.

'Okay. We will give you a few minutes to take this photo opportunity, then we will continue.'

Turning he said, 'Elizabeth, have you enough handouts for the press? There seems to be rather a lot of them.'

'Yes, Robert, I ran off an extra batch this morning.'

'Mr Thomas, I expect some questions of a political nature will be asked. Can you handle them?'

'Certainty, Mr Kilpatrick, that's why I have been sent here. It's a delicate situation for the Government, having the PM isolated from power.'

'OK, I think they have had long enough. Let's continue.'

Robert called them to order. 'Everyone return to your seat, please, and we will continue. The visiting party are trapped behind a fall of rock and rubble that we estimate to be about 150 yards long. The visitors are safe, and reasonably well, with plenty of drinking water, and the undermanager, Tommy Green — a very experienced mining engineer — is in charge, and looking after them. There is a good supply of fresh air and Tommy has determined that the gas levels there are low. The Mines Rescue team are in attendance, at the face of the fall, along with medical facilities. Redman's foreman blacksmith has, over the last twenty-four hours, with his team, designed and built a rescue tube that I will now explain.'

Standing, he turned to remove the black cloth from the blackboard.

'Now, there is no need to go crazy taking photos, as I have produced a detailed hand-out for you all, which Miss Hardy will give you later.'

On the board was pinned a large-scale drawing of the rescue tube, which had been produced by the coal board's draughtsman from the chalk drawing in the blacksmiths shop. The drawing showed the tube and its operation through the various stages.

Robert continued, 'The BBC has had access to this drawing beforehand, and their production technicians, have produced a graphic video tape showing the tube in use, which they will now show.'

The projection screen suddenly lit up, as the video started to play.

It showed, in a graphic form, the tube and its assembly, and depicted the rescue men climbing into it, excavating and removing the rubble using the cart.

The video then showed the fitters operating the rams to inch forward the tube further into the fall area. Then, optimistically, it showed the rescue team breaking through and placing casualties onto the cart to be pulled to safety on the other side of the fall.

When the film finished the room was silent until one person started to clap. Immediately everyone else joined in.

'Okay, I would like to thank the BBC for that enlightening film, which I understand is to be broadcast, by the BBC, with every news bulletin and, due to the international interest, also on their world service.Now we will allow ten minutes for any questions.'

A well-known BBC presenter stood up, holding a microphone. 'Can I ask the Government representative what is happening to the security of the country whilst the Prime Minister is trapped underground?'

David Thomas, clearing his throat, replied in an upper-class, superior accent, 'Well, as per the Government's laid down procedure, the Foreign Secretary, as Deputy Prime Minister, has taken control in Number 10 Downing Street and, thanks to the arrangements made by Colliery Manager Mr Sankey, on a number of occasions has been able to speak and concur with the Prime Minister via a special secure communications link through the mine's underground telephone system. So the governing of the country, during this crisis, is functioning normally. The people of Great Britain have nothing to fear.'

A reporter from one of the tabloid newspapers jumped to his feet, and shouted, 'Talking about the Colliery Manager, why did he not accompany this party, instead of staying in his office on the surface? Did he suspect something that nobody else did?'

Robert Kilpatrick stood up to answer and, taking a deep breath, answered, in a stern and defensive manner, 'Mr Sankey, is suffering from a fractured ankle, so physically he was unable to accompany the party. But I can tell you that, despite his painful disability, he has insisted on leading the rescue effort. Such is his dedicated that he is at present underground at the trapped area, directing operations.'

Robert then sat down and stared angrily at the questioner.

Another pressman stood up and, in a more relaxed voice, asked, 'How are the trapped men and when will the rescuers break through?'

Standing again, Robert replied, 'The Deputy Coal Board Chairman is seriously injured, and at the moment unconscious but stable. The rest of the group have minor injuries and, as I stated earlier, the undermanager, Tommy Green, a fully-trained and experienced first-aider, is in charge. As to the second part of your question,we expect to break through within the next twenty-four hours. Right, I think that is enough for now. Thank you very much for attending this briefing. Don't forget to collect details of the rescue tube from Miss Hardy, on your way out.'

The press then rushed to leave the building, in an effort to lodge their stories before their respective news deadlines.

'Good morning, Prime Minister. Did you have a good sleep?'

'No, Tommy, I just cat-napped through the night. How

are you?'

'Oh, I can manage with little sleep these days. I often get woken up during the night, when the pit has production difficulties during the night shift.'

'Goodness, and here's me thinking a PM's job is difficult. How is our casualty doing today?'

'I am a bit worried. His breathing is a bit ragged at the moment. I'm going to have a chat to Drew, your security guard. Did you know he was trained as a medic by the army?'

'Yes, when he was assigned to me I knew Drew Martin was trained as a medic. Obviously we had a full security vetting on him. Not only has he been medically trained but he did one year as a medical student at Manchester University, but had to drop out when his father suddenly died. He had to help his mother bring up his four younger brothers and his sister. That's why, when he qualified for the SAS, they jumped at the chance to train him in medical skills.'

'Okay, Sir, I'll go and ask his advice, and get him to look at the casualty.'

'Right, Tommy. Keep me informed.'

Tommy walked over to where Drew was sitting with his back leaned against a pile of timber supplies.

'Hi, Drew. Drew, now that is an unusual name.'

'Yes, Tommy, it's short for Andrew, but everyone calls me Drew. Except in the regiment, where it's Drew Drop.'

'Drew Drop? Why?'

'Well, we were once on an exercise in Germany, and I accidentally dropped a live grenade. You should have seen everyone move! Somehow, I managed to scramble and scoop it up, and throw it safely to the other side of the training area. I got a right bollocking, and ever since it's been Drew

156

Drop.'

'Phew, a close shave, eh? The PM was telling me that you started training as a doctor, but had to pull out.'

'Yes, sad that, but family comes first. I couldn't let my mother struggle bringing up my brothers and sister. That's one reason why when they grew up I joined the Army as soon as I could. When I passed selection for the SAS, I jumped at the opportunity to take extra training as a medic. As part of that training I spent six months working in the Accident and Emergency Department at Queen's Hospital, Nottingham, where I acquired some amazing new skills. Later they sent me to the USA to train with the Navy Seals medical unit. They are brilliant and employ the latest battlefield medical emergency techniques. When my time was up with the SAS, I was not happy returning to an ordinary regiment, after the excitement of operations.'

After taking a quick drink of water, Drew continued, 'Then out of the blue, this job came up, so I jumped at it. Although, I was extensively trained in weapons, I would basically become a policeman, therefore, I had to attend Police training college. I even spent twelve months on the beat on London's streets, before being accepted in the Royal Diplomatic Protection Service. I get on well with the Prime Minister, but some of the Cabinet can be a bit snotty. I've settled well in the job, apart from this week, but I often wish I had been able to complete my medical studies and become a doctor.'

'Well now, that's the main reason that I came over, Drew,' said Tommy. 'I'm a bit worried about the Deputy Chairman's condition. Will you come over and give me your opinion?'

They both went over to the casualty and knelt down beside him.

'Tommy, I can see why you were worried about him. His

breathing is very shallow, and his face is pale. I think shock is setting in.'

Drew placed his fingers near the casualty's throat to feel his pulse.

'His pulse is there Tommy, but very feeble.'

Suddenly, the casualty gave a gasp and stopped breathing.

Tommy jumped up. 'Quick, Drew. Help me to turn him over, so I can start Artificial Resuscitation.'

'Tommy, I know you were trained in the Holger Nielson respiration technique, but, the American Navy Seals taught me a brand new technique which they called mouth-to-mouth resuscitation. Stand back. I will deal with this.'

Drew quickly, placed one hand under the casualty's neck and the other on his forehead. He then tilted the head back as far as it would go.

'Now, Tommy,' Drew said. 'With his head back like this it opens up a clear airway.'

He pinched the casualty's nostrils and, holding his chin down with his other hand, Drew then took a deep breath, and completely covered the casualty's mouth with his own mouth. He blew into the casualty's mouth five times in quick succession, lifting his head each time to take in a gulp of fresh air.

Tommy looked on in amazement.

Drew raised his head, counted five seconds, then got into a rhythm of one breath every five seconds.

After about three minutes, the Deputy Chairman suddenly coughed and spluttered. Drew stopped immediately. Both Drew and Tommy were very relieved when the casualty started breathing regularly, and steadily, on his own.

'God, Drew, that was amazing. I can't believe that was possible. It's a miracle.'

'Yes, Tommy, it is pretty amazing. But I have only ever carried it out on a dummy.

You know, I predict it is only a matter of time before every first-aider in the world will be using that technique, it's so easy. Now, help me to put him in the recovery position, in case he's sick.'

With that, the two men turned him over into the prone position.

'Right, we've done what we can for now, so let's sit here and monitor his condition. An you can tell me how you got to be Undermanager.'

So Tommy outlined his progress in the industry from leaving school.


At the rescue site the rescue team leader was speaking to the assembled group.

'Right, get that man out of the tube now, he has had his twenty minutes of intensive digging. Roundall, you're a big lad. Get your arse in there and take over for the next stint.'

'Aye, all reet. But I can do more than twenty minutes. Easily.'

'No, Roundall, that's an order. We don't need any more tragedies. When I say out, you come out, okay?'

'Okay, boss.'

As the man emerged from the tube, Roundall entered and took his place. He soon had the first tub filled and shouted for it to be dragged back and emptied.

The team had driven into the fall by twenty full tubes, which left only ten or so to go.

Suddenly the telephone rang and Bill Sankey hobbled over to answer it.

After listening for a few minutes, he hung the earpiece back on its hook and limped back over, shaking his head.

'Annie,' he shouted. 'Developments. Tommy just informed me that the Deputy Chairman stopped breathing and Drew, the PM's security guard, performed, according to Tommy, some sort of a miracle by something called mouth-to-mouth. I think that's what he said.'

'Ah, Mr Sankey, I have read about that,' said Annie. 'It's a new form of resusitation and has been developed in America. It's supposed to be very effective and easy to do after very little training. I must have a word with this Drew.'

'So, he's okay now, but I'd better make sure my oxygen kit is fully functioning.'

After twenty minutes Roundall was ordered out of the tube and replaced by another rescue worker.

Unbelievably, due to Roundall's tremendous efforts, two more full tubes had been extended into the fall.


The men all turned when they heard a group of men approaching. The men were carrying large cardboard boxes.

'Ey up, lads. Pies have come,' shouted Harry, the rescue's resident comic.

The pies and hot tea were distributed among the team and they were devoured greedily.

Harry exclaimed, 'God, there's nothing like a steaming hot pie, and by God these are good. I remember when I was doing my National Service, we were in the middle of the Malaysian jungle, six of us squaddies, sat round having a brew. I started to relate how good Nuttall's meat pies were, describing slowly how, when you took a bite when it was piping hot, how the hot piece of pie burned your mouth and you had to suck cool air in. And then the great taste of the meat and succulent pastry taste hit your senses. Then half-way through, how you would tilt your head back, and noisily suck the pie's warm gravy juices out. As you did this, inevitably some would run down your arm inside your sleeve, making your arm all sticky. Messy, but God, what a treat. Suddenly, we heard a deep sobbing. We turned to look at a big sixteen-stone giant of a soldier, crying like a baby, sobbing like mad, "What's to do," I shouted at him. "Oh, Harry!" he cried. "I could taste that pie. I could even feel the gravy running down my arm! I'm homesick! I want that pie."'.

The whole rescue team burst out laughing at Harry's story; it had certainly broken the sombre mood, a mood brought on by the task ahead.


Suitably refreshed the men set about the task with a renewed energy.

Some five weary hours later they suddenly broke through, and a loud cheer went up on both sides of the fall.

The Captain ordered the last man out and Bill Sankey then took over.

'Well done, lads, fantastic effort. Now, Annie, I want you to go through with me and examine the party. I will go first and you follow me.'

'Excuse me, Mr Sankey,' enquired Roundall.

'Could I go through with you and carry Annie's medical equipment? I am a trained first-aider.'

The Manager could not help but to have noticed the close relationship that had developed between Annie and Roundall, and replied, 'Okay, Roundall, you follow me with the medical supplies. Annie, you follow Roundall.'

Annie smiled at Roundall and gave his arm a little squeeze.

The Manager climbed into the tube, followed by Roundall and Annie brought up the rear.


A few minutes later Bill Sankey emerged from the other end of the tube, slowly stood up and limped over to where Tommy and the other men were congregated. He stopped and surveyed the scene in front of him.

Tommy ran forward and, with tears in his eyes, gave Bill Sankey a big bear-hug.

'By God, Bill, am I glad to see thee.'

'Same here, Tommy. What a couple of days this has been.'

Just then, Roundall emerged from the tube, grinning.

'I don't believe it, Roundall, thy gets everywhere,' Tommy exclaimed.

'Aye, I thought I should help get the old bugger out, knowing thy Mabel would never forgive me.' Come here, lad.' He gave Roundall another big hug.

'Right, Annie, do your stuff. And let's get these good people out of here,' said Bill.


Twenty minutes later, after Annie had established that the major casualty was comfortable, and had treated the other minor wounds, the rescue team carefully loaded the Deputy Chairman onto the trolley and strapped him on using thick leather belts. He was then carefully pulled through the tube, and immediately, carried out by stretcher to the cage and hence to the surface where an Ambulance was waiting. Within an hour he was being admitted to Wigan Infirmary.

An hour later, the VIPs, along with Annie, had been taken through the tube and were now on their way to the surface, but Annie remained at the entrance of the tube, awaiting her hero.

The rescue tube had been a complete success.

The Prime Minister had insisted that he be one of the last to leave.

This left him, along with Drew, Bill Sankey, Roundall and Tommy, still to go through the tube.

They were pulling the trolley back, when suddenly a loud crack was heard from the roof area near to the tube exit.

'STOP! get back, screamed Bill. 'The roof's caving.'

They all jumped back, away from the tube, and waited, hearing the trickle and creak of the rock strata.

After awhile, all was quiet again, and they slowly crept back to examine the area.

Looking up, Tommy exclaimed, 'My goodness, look at the size of that rock!'

They all looked to where Tommy was pointing and saw a massive piece of sandstone hanging precariously above the tube entrance.

'Right, lads,' Bill ordered. 'I will get on the phone, and get some timber sent through, so we can build up a support structure to prevent it falling.'

Roundall interrupted. 'Hang on, Mr Sankey, I don't think we have much time left before it moves. I don't think the timber will be here quick enough. Tell you what, I will brace myself up between the rock and the floor, and you lot get out quick.'

'Don't be daft, Roundall. I know thy are a big strong lad, but if that moves it will flatten thee,' said Tommy.

'Nay, Tommy, I'm not that stupid. You all get out now, and send a rescue man back straightaway, with any timber that's left, and he can pack it under the stone, whilst I get free from under it. Honestly, go. I know I can do this. This way there's only me at risk. Go on, get going,' he shouted.

Ignoring their doubt about the action, Roundall moved towards the stone and gently positioned his broad shoulders under it. 'Come on! Move your arses, we've not got all day'

Reluctantly, looking back at Roundall with concern, they climbed out through the tube. When they emerged and explained the developments to Annie, she was very fearful.

When the three of them had gone, the place became deadly quiet. Roundall crouched beneath the stone, sweating profusely.

Just when he was thinking how stupid he was, a man's head popped out of the tube. Harry, the joker of the rescue party, burst out laughing when he saw Roundall. 'Blooming heck, Roundall. I wish I had a camera, you just look like that Greek God, what's his name? Ah, Atlas — with the world on his shoulders.'

'Get over here, you daft sod and spragg this thing before it flattens me.'

Harry dragged over the timber he had brought through the tube and

after ten minutes he'd built a stacked structure tight under the rock. Roundall carefully eased himself from under it and they both stood back as the rock creakily settled on the structure.

Roundall shook Harry's hand and said, 'Come on, mate, let's get out of here, quick.'

They both scrabbled through the tube.

As they emerged at the other end, a cheer went out from all the team and they all started to slap the men on their backs.

Annie couldn't help herself, and she rushed forward and

with a tearful eye threw her arms around Roundall's neck and gave him a big kiss.

All Roundall's mates cheered and Harry then asked, 'Annie, I'm next, eh?'

Just as they were leaving the area they heard a loud whoosh, as the stone and the roof at the other side of the tube collapsed.

'Phew, it's your lucky day, Roundall,' said Harry. 'As well as getting the girl.'


As they rose slowly in the cage, they could see crowds waiting on the surface. They emerged from the cage and on reaching the bottom of the steps, a great cheer went up from the assembled crowd. A mass of reporters and photographers ran forward, flash bulbs going off continuously. The media were in frenzy.

A number of policemen ran forward and dragged them to the side to allow the party through.

The Prime Minister turned to the reporters, 'Okay, I know you all want a comment, but give me half an hour to get myself together and I promise you we will have a full press conference. Now please excuse us.'

The party, with a policeman escorting them, walked slowly toward the Manager's office. A large number of workers and their families lined their way and started to cheer and clap them as they walked through.

A few yards from the manager's office, Ivy and her girls, in their best clean, white pinnies, were lined up, and as Bill was level with Ivy, they all smartly saluted him.

Bill, looked straight at Ivy's smiling radiant face, and she gave him a big cheeky wink.

# Twenty-Three

The government cars started to arrive at Claridge's Hotel for the formal dinner. All those who had been trapped in the mine were expected to be present.

Roundall and Annie and Tommy and his wife Mabel were already at the hotel as they had been staying there for the last three days, as personal guests of the Prime Minister.

They strolled into the lounge for pre-dinner drinks as it was slowly starting to fill up with the arriving guests.

They were greeted by Robert Kilpatrick, who was arm-in-arm with Elizabeth Hardy. Smiling, Robert extended his hand. 'Hello, it's great to see you all.'

Tommy shook his hand warmly. 'I understand congratulations are in order, as I have been just told you two got married last week here in London. Congratulations and good luck to you both.'

Annie let a out a barely-hidden giggle. 'Oh, Elizabeth, let me have a look at your rings, please.'

Elizabeth held up her left hand to show a large diamond engagement ring and a simple, broad gold wedding band.

'My goodness, look at that diamond. It's a whopper and so beautiful.'

'Yes, Annie, it's a family heirloom and was Robert's late grandmother's. I love it.'

Annie gave Elizabeth a nudge and winked at her saying, 'Well I have good news, too. Roundall proposed to me last night, and I said yes.'

They both grabbed each other and started jumping up and down, both laughing.

'Wonderful, Annie, you are a perfect couple,' Elizabeth said, smiling at Roundall who was blushing silently.

Robert, breaking Roundall's embarrassment said, 'Come on, let's take a seat over there on those big leather sofas.'

So they all took their drinks over to two large Chesterfield sofas near the window, and after a short white the colliery manager Bill Sankey joined them.

Several members of the cabinet, who had been involved in the incident, were circulating around the room and chatting to various groups.

Tommy was sitting facing the entrance door to the lounge, when suddenly, his face lit up with a beaming smile as Drew Martin entered the room.

'Drew, over here,' shouted Tommy. 'Look, everyone, it's Drew Drop Martin!' he said, as Drew and he exchanged a warm handshake.

'Ah, Drew it's great to see you. Are you still carrying a gun for the PM?'

'Great news, on that front, Tommy. I'm now a second-year medical student at Guy's Hospital, thanks to the Prime Minister's influence.

They accepted my previous medical training and I was allowed to skip the first year. I'm loving it.'

'Wonderful news, Drew. Let me know when you qualify and we'll come down for it.'

'Tommy, you and Mabel will be my chief guests of honour at my graduation.'

He then turned to the remainder of the group and they hugged and chatted happily.

Suddenly, the room went quiet, and everyone turned to see the Prime Minister enter the room. He stopped, looked around, and on seeing Tommy's group strode towards them.

'Well, here are the heros, I owe you lot a great amount.'

Roundall stood up. 'Thank you very much, Prime Minister, and thank you for your kind hospitality in putting us up in this splendid hotel.'

Just then a uniformed porter entered and announced, 'Ladies and Gentlemen, dinner is about to be served. Please proceed to the dining room.'

The friends felt that the whole dinner was a great success, and the meal one of the finest they had ever had, although they were a little embarrassed at the praise given out to them during the after-dinner speeches.


Earlier that morning, at precisely eleven o'clock, Tommy, Mabel, Roundall and Annie had attended a special award ceremony at Buckingham Palace, where Her Majesty The Queen had awarded Tommy an OBE for his gallant effort in taking charge and looking after the trapped visitors. Roundall had been awarded the British Empire Medal for his bravery during the rescue.


It was now just going dark and Tommy, Mabel, Roundall, Annie, Robert and Elizabeth were standing at the top end of The Mall, looking down at the illuminated Palace.

Annie made them all link arms as they strolled down the Mall, striding out in step, and singing, 'Any old iron, any old iron, any any any old iron, you look sweet, talk about a treat...', then they couldn't sing any more as they burst out laughing. They moved to sit on a low wall at the side of the Mall.

As the six friends sat there, reflecting on the hectic day, sighing, Annie said, 'Haven't we come a long way?'

'Aye,' Roundall agreed.

'Who would have thought it, Tommy Thunder OBE. Mabel, you must have been really proud at the Palace, when the Queen gave him that medal.'

Mabel was quiet for a few seconds then replied, 'Aye, I was, lad, reet proud of him, as he approached the Queen. But I nearly died when I saw he had odd socks on.'

Immediately, as one, they all looked down at Tommy's feet, to see he was indeed wearing a brown sock on one foot, and a black one on the other.

They all suddenly burst out laughing, including Tommy and Mabel.

They knew, from that day on, this image would stay in their memory forever.

# Twenty-Four

Ten years later, Redman's Colliery was still producing good quality household coal and was showing a healthy profit.

Its new Colliery Manager, Frank Taylor, had just started, having being somewhat surprised to have landed this particular healthy Colliery post so early on in his career, He loved this pit, and had fond memories of his time spent here learning his trade.

His appointment was probably helped by the newly appointed Area General Manager, Bill Sankey – Redman's last successful manager, who was very familiar with Frank's potential and ability.

Tommy Green OBE was still Redman's Undermanager and knew Frank was a good appointment.

Tommy had been offered promotion by the Coal Board to a desk job at the Divisional Headquarters, but he had declined. As he had confided in his devoted wife, Mabel, 'I know pit work, it's what I am best at, and I would be bored stiff sat behind a desk.'

At which Mabel had agreed, saying, 'Aye, Tommy, best stick to what thy knows best, being pit brunt!'

Dan, the Foreman Blacksmith had now retired, and he and his wife had bought a bungalow in North Wales, where he planned to do a lot of beach fishing in the Irish Sea.

His invention of the rescue tube had been taken up by a leading mining equipment manufacturer and was now a vital part in mines rescue operations. Dan was engaged as a part-time consultant on equipment development, for which he received a generous annual retainer. His retirement presentation at the Colliery had been a grand event, with even the top brass from the Division attending. His dear friend, Ivy, and her team had put on a great spread.

Bill Sankey had presented Dan with some fabulous beach fishing equipment and gave a touching speech. After the formal presentations, Dan's number one blacksmith, Freddy, Senior Blacksmith, who was taking over the reigns from Dan, presented him with a beautifully made working model of the rescue tubes, complete with working rams, encased in a mahogany case which his workshop had made, in secret, over the previous few months. Dan, for once, was lost for words and, hiding a tear, he paused to light a full strength cigarette whilst he gathered his thoughts, to allow him to thank them properly.

Billy was now twenty-six years old and had developed into a strapping, fit young man. As coal extraction had become fully mechanised over the last ten years, Billy was now working on the coalface and operated a monster of a coal-cutting machine, whose large round drum, fitted with hundreds of sharp steel picks, shattered the coal seam, as it rotated and advanced parallel along the face, sending tons of coal out on the steel link conveyor. Billy, although now one of the pit's top colliers, and earning really good money, had not lost his caring, straightforward manner and was well-liked by all the miners at the pit.

Billy's dad, Johnny, still worked at the mine but, like many of his generation in the industry, had suffered many knocks and bumps and had now changed to much lighter work, carrying out essential conveyor maintenance. Johnny and his wife, Edna, were really proud of the way their son Billy had turned out.

Ivy had taken early retirement to open a café in the nearby town, which now had the reputation of making the best bacon baps in town. A lot of her old mining customers regularly visited the café, especially on a Saturday. Nellie, recently married to a mines rescuer, had taken over as Canteen Manageress and had maintained Ivy's high standards.

One shadow over the mine was the recent imprisonment of Dick Wayne. The Baths Superintendent had for some months suspected that someone was stealing small amounts of money, on a regular basis, from the miners' lockers, but had been unable to catch the culprit. Along with Robert Kilpatrick and help from the local CID officer, he had set up a trap for the thief, by placing marked coins and notes in clothes in a miner's clean locker. Three days later the CID officer had stopped Dick Wayne as he left the baths and escorted him back into the Superintendent's office where a search of his pockets had revealed the marked money. Dick was subsequently arrested and charged and later sent to prison for two months by the local magistrates. Although not liked by most of the miners, they were shocked that one amongst them could stoop so low as to steal from his work colleagues.

Life for Roundall, however, had taken a totally unexpected turn after his part in the rescue. He had returned from his award at the Palace to a hero's welcome by the town. The

National Union of Mine Workers had persuaded him to put his name forward to the local Labour selection committee as a candidate for the forthcoming General Election. The decision to choose him was a unanimous vote by the Committee.Not surprisingly, in this Northern mining town, he won with a massive increased majority. He had been the town's sitting MP for eight years now, being re-elected partway through the period. Due to his mining experience he was a good, knowledgeable voice for all the miners throughout the country. He lived with his wife of nine years, Nurse Annie Belshaw, in a semi-detached house on the outskirts of town with their two children, Annie aged seven and Dan, five.

He also had the use of a London flat, owned by the Kilpatrick Estate, for when he was sitting in the House of Commons. He spent most of the week there when parliament was sitting, returning home each Thursday night on the Inter City Express.


As for Robert Kilpatrick, he had now left mining, having been finally persuaded by his family to take over as Chief Executive of their Merchant Bank on the retirement of his father, who stayed on as Chairman of the Board, allowing him to keep his eye one his son's handling of the bank's business. Robert and Elizabeth had bought a large house in Mayfair and although, as yet, they had no children, they were still very much in love and blissfully happy.


The Prime Minister, Charles Thornton, lost the last election to Labour and had decided that the time had come to retire. He had subsequently been elevated to the House of Lords.


Sir Alf Kenyon, Deputy Chairman, never really recovered from the injuries sustained in the mine and, after a long illness, passed away in his London home surrounded by his family. He was given a large funeral, jointly paid for by the NCB and the Government. The Prime Minister had attended, and it was held in the magnificent Durham Cathedral, Sir Alf's hometown, the service being lead by the Anglican Bishop of Durham, with the Prime Minister saying a few words during the service.

So, the group were dispersed far and wide and although Robert and Elizabeth often saw Roundall in London they had little contact with the others. They had, however, vowed to have a reunion every five years, on the anniversary date of the rescue.

Four years ago they had held the first such reunion dinner, at Lambert Jones's Manor House Hotel in Wigan, where the six close friends — Roundall and Annie, Tommy and Mabel, and Robert and Elizabeth — had been joined by Bill Sankey and his wife Sheila, Dan and his wife Mary and finally Doctor Drew (Drop) Martin. Lambert had arranged that Wigan's celebrated French chef prepare a special eight-course meal. The meal and reunion was a great success. Later the friends were having a quiet brandy, sitting in the ornate coffee lounge and Roundall, now used to public speaking, stood up and said, 'Ladies and Gentlemen, nay, Friends, please raise your glasses for a toast. The toast is Dan and his Rescue Tube.'

'Dan and his Rescue tube,' they echoed.

Lambert was excitedly already planning the next five-year reunion event.